TOM HUDDLESTON

A long time ago in a galaxy far, far away . . . .

THE RESCUE

It is a time of darkness. With the end of the Clone Wars and the destruction of the Jedi Order, the evil Emperor Palpatine rules the galaxy unopposed.

After months of searching, Milo and Lina Graf have learned that their parents, Rhyssa and Auric, are being held in an Imperial mining colony on the planet Agaris, deep in Wild Space.

Travelling in a stolen Imperial transport, Milo and Lina have come to Agaris determined to free their parents from the clutches of the Empire. But on this mist-shrouded world, nothing is as it seems....

CHAPTER 1

AGARIS

The anchoring spike shot out from the *Star Herald*'s underside, burrowing deep into the surface of the tiny moon. This rock was barely worthy of the name, Lina thought to herself – it wasn't so much a moon as a misshapen meteor, caught by the planet's gravity and doomed to orbit endlessly. Still, it should be enough to hide them.

Milo hit the recoil switch and the cable drew taut, securing the stolen Imperial ship in place. CR-8R cut the power and the cockpit was plunged into darkness. Morq burrowed down into Milo's lap, chittering softly.

'Nice move, sis,' Milo breathed. 'Crate, did they see us?'

CR-8R shook his metal head. 'There has been no detectable increase in Imperial chatter,' he said. 'It would appear that Miss Lina's quick thinking has allowed us to arrive unnoticed.'

Lina peered out through the viewport as the pale light of dawn leaked into the cockpit. 'Now the question is, how do we get from here to there?'

Above the moon's desolate surface, the planet Agaris was rising. A gloomy, forbidding world, it was shrouded in shifting banks of murky cloud. But even in those small patches where the cloud cover broke, Lina could see none of the dazzling greens and blues she would've expected from a world like this. Agaris was teeming with life – all their sensors said so. But beneath the grey all she could see was more grey.

‘The Imperial compound is located on the northernmost continent,’ CR-8R said, pointing with a long metal finger. ‘Sensors read a powerful energy signal.’

‘Just one base?’ Milo asked, surprised. ‘Mira and Ephraim said the Empire had been taking over whole worlds, setting up base after base so they could control the population.’

‘Maybe there’s no population to control,’ Lina pointed out. ‘There’s no sign of any cities or technology.’

‘Master Milo has a point, though,’ CR-8R said. ‘If Agaris is the site of an Imperial mining operation, why do the sensors pick up no drilling sites or auxiliary bases beyond the central compound? That said, it does help us in one important respect: there is only one place your parents could possibly be.’

Milo reached for Lina’s hand and together they gazed at the vast pale globe. Somewhere up there Rhyssa and Auric Graf were waiting, imprisoned and unsuspecting. Their long search was almost at an end.

Lina tried to picture her parents' faces, tried to summon up the smell of them and the sound of their voices. In recent weeks these things had begun to fade, her dreams of Rhyssa and Auric drowned out by darkness and danger. But no longer, she promised herself. Soon, somehow, they would all be back together. She and Milo would find a way. They had to.

A glimmer in the blackness caught her eye, and she felt Milo's grip tighten. The Star Destroyer *Executrix* glided from the planet's shadow like a sleek silver shark, hunting for prey. The command tower emerged into the light, bristling with laser turrets and antennae.

'Are you absolutely *sure* they can't see us?' Milo asked nervously.

'All of the *Star Herald*'s systems have been powered down,' CR-8R told him. 'We are a grey ship on a grey moon. And they have no idea we are here.'

'Let's hear them anyway, Crate,' Lina suggested. 'Just in case.'

'I assure you, Mistress Lina,' CR-8R said, a little defensively. 'I am monitoring all Imperial transmissions, if anything out of the ordinary . . .'

'We trust you, Crater,' Milo said. 'It'll just make us feel better, is all.'

'You'll feel better listening to the voices of your enemy?' CR-8R asked. 'Sometimes I simply do not understand the two of you.'

But he patched the signal through nonetheless, the hiss of static rattling through the *Star Herald*'s internal speakers. It had been an unwitting gift from the ship's previous owner, Captain Korda – a scanner pre-tuned to all the Imperial communication bands, even a few classified ones. When this was over, Lina thought, they could hand the ship over to Mira and Ephraim Bridger, back on Lothal. Perhaps their friends would forgive them for running away.

'*Executrix, this is transport three-six-six,*' a voice came through, distant and distorted. '*We're ready for departure.*'

'*Roger that, three-six-six,*' a second man replied. '*Prepare to release docking clamps.*'

A bulky haulage vessel emerged from the Destroyer's ventral hangar, flanked by a pair of TIE fighters. Engines flared and the three ships moved towards the planet, a trio of black specks silhouetted against the clouds.

'*Agaris base, we have locked onto your beacon and are making our descent,*' the first voice said as the transport vanished into the murky atmosphere. '*Escort, keep your eyes peeled for those stalks.*'

Milo looked at Lina, confused. 'Stalks?' he asked. 'Like, plant stalks?'

'Or storks?' Lina suggested. 'Maybe some kind of giant bird down there?'

'They'd have to be pretty huge to take down an Imperial transport,' Milo said. 'Either way, it's weird.'

'Executrix, *this is C-patrol,*' a clearer voice cut in, and Lina ducked instinctively as a second pair of TIEs shrieked overhead, angling towards the Destroyer. '*We've finished our sweep, there are no ships out here. Whatever happened to those men it's the compound's problem, not ours.*'

'*Stow that talk, C-patrol,*' a voice replied abruptly. '*Or I'll have you reassigned to planetary scout duty. How would you like that?*'

'R-roger that, Executrix,*'* the pilot replied. *'Um, please inform Governor Tarkin that our sensors are clean. But we'll do another sweep just in case.'*

'That's better, C-patrol,' the officer said. *'Make this a double shift and perhaps we can forget about your . . . inappropriate comment.'*

'Tarkin,' Milo said. 'I've heard that name. Ephraim said he was a big noise in the Imperial high command.'

'So what's he doing all the way out here?' Lina asked. 'And what were they talking about, what happened to their men?'

'Maybe it's those giant storks,' Milo mused. 'Maybe they ate them!'

'The pilot implied that the incident was still a mystery,' CR-8R put in. 'Clearly the situation on Agaris is far from satisfactory, from an Imperial standpoint.'

'Which could be good for us,' Lina said. 'If they're distracted by these storks or whatever, it'll make it easier for us to sneak in.'

'If this Tarkin is as important as Master Milo believes, he will be well guarded,' the droid told her.

Milo nodded. 'But if they're so busy guarding him, maybe they won't pay so much attention to a couple of prisoners.'

Lina grinned. 'Right,' she said. 'Let's get down there and find out.'

They watched in silence as the *Executrix* crossed the face of the planet, a black arrow against the swirling clouds. The moon drifted on an opposite orbit, taking them gradually out of range. Soon the Star Destroyer had been swallowed by the grey face of Agaris.

'Once we've detached I'll give her two seconds of thrust,' Lina explained. 'That should be enough to break the moon's orbit and enter the planet's gravity. Crater, leave all other systems shut down until we reach the cover of those clouds.'

'All of them?' the droid asked. 'But Mistress Lina, with no way to navigate we will be in a blind spin, you will have no way to –'

'Let me worry about that, Crate,' she said. 'With luck, anyone watching will think we're just a hunk of debris. Milo, retract the anchor. Let's move before that Star Destroyer comes back around.'

She felt the *Star Herald* lifting gently off the moon's surface, and heard a clunk as the cable snaked back into the ship. 'Crater, bring the engines back on line,' Lina ordered. 'Three, two . . . '

And she hit the thrusters, the little moon's gravity tugging them back in their seats as the *Star Herald* rose, her snub nose pointed directly at the dim world below.

Seconds later Lina cut the power, hoping no Imperial observers had spotted the brief flare of their engines. She felt the planet's gravity take hold, a steady downward pull. The *Star Herald* began to roll, Agaris sliding slowly out of view, replaced first by star-studded space then by the lumpy, uneven cylinder of the little moon, receding behind them.

Milo groaned. 'I shouldn't have eaten the last of that icefish for breakfast.'

'Try shutting your eyes,' Lina suggested.

Milo tried it for a moment, then shook his head. 'That just makes it worse.'

They could see Agaris again now, filling the screen with shifting masses of grey. Their spin was starting to speed up, the planet's gravity tugging them in every direction at once. Morq gave a sickly moan. Lina knew how he felt.

'Executrix, *this is C-patrol.*' The pilot's voice was suddenly back, and Lina jerked her head up. 'Executrix, *come in please.*'

'*This is* Executrix,' the officer's voice replied. '*What is it now, C-patrol?*'

'*We're making our second pass,*' the pilot said. '*We've picked up something on the scanners. Sending the report now.*'

Lina looked back at Milo, barely daring to speak. As the *Star Herald* rolled they could see the fighters, distant but closing.

The officer sighed. '*We appreciate your diligence, C-patrol, but there's no need to report every meteorite your scanners pick up.*'

'*It's made of metal, sir,*' the pilot radioed back. '*I know there are no power readings but –*'

'*So it's a meteorite with an iron core,*' the officer interrupted. '*Or it's a hunk of space debris, probably from last time we dumped the garbage. Ignore it, C-patrol, and continue your sweep.'*

Lina breathed relief. That had been much too close. If the Empire spotted them now, they'd be finished. Even if they managed to escape, they'd have lost the element of surprise.

The *Star Herald* rolled towards the planet, and now she could see high cloud turrets reaching up towards them. Once they were safely inside the atmosphere she'd fire up the thrusters and find somewhere to land. 'Crater,' she said. 'Get ready to –'

'Executrix, *we're going to check it out,'* the pilot's voice crashed into the cockpit. '*You're probably right, but it's my neck if the Governor finds out we missed something important.'*

Milo's face whitened. Lina gripped the arm rests.

'Very well, C-patrol,' the officer replied. *'But make it fast.'*

'Crater, get her started,' Lina barked. 'Milo, strap in tight.'

She felt the engines rattle and catch and slammed the thrusters, turning that sickening roll into a twisting dive. She could imagine the look of surprise on the TIE pilot's face as the drifting hunk of space debris suddenly flared into life, rocketing towards the planet.

'They're coming after us,' Milo warned her.

'I'm sure they are,' Lina replied as they plunged into the atmosphere, the air paling from black to blue.

Then the clouds swallowed them. One moment they were streaking down in bright sunlight, the next they were ploughing through a dense fog, trails of vapour streaming across the screen. Winds buffeted the *Star Herald*'s hull

and the ship rattled as Lina hauled back on the steering bar, levelling them out.

They broke from the clouds into the gloom of a murky day. The sun was a watery glow behind the clouds, and below them Lina could see a dark plain stretching to a range of jagged mountains on the distant horizon.

At first she thought the surface was bare – just smooth grey-brown rocks. Then, looking closer, she saw that it was covered with huge domes, like blisters on the skin of Agaris. 'Are those . . . ' she asked, perplexed. 'They look like . . . '

'Mushrooms,' Milo finished for her. 'A whole forest of them. And they're huge – look at that one, it's bigger than the ship.'

'Giant fungi are not uncommon – they are found on many charted worlds,' CR-8R pointed out.

'But there doesn't seem to be anything else,' Milo said. 'Where are the trees, where's the grass? It's just mushrooms every–'

There was a roar, and the *Star Herald* shook violently. Morq gave a shriek, jumping from Milo's lap and shivering beneath the navigation console. Lina slammed the steering bar sideways and the next blast just missed them, a green bolt flashing past into the mushroom forest below.

'We cannot evade them, Mistress Lina,' CR-8R said. 'They are following too closely behind us.'

Checking the rear viewport, Lina saw that he was right. The two TIEs were almost on them, their ion engines roaring. Evasive manoeuvres would be no use at all at this range – so where were they going to go?

'What's that?' Milo asked, pointing up ahead. 'It looks like a tower.'

A tall shape was outlined against the sky. Milo was right, it did look like an artificial structure: a slender black skyscraper with a wide base.

'Imperial?' Lina asked.

'The Imperial compound is still some distance away, at the base of those mountains,' CR-8R said. 'And this structure does not correspond to any design I am familiar with.'

Another blast hit the ship, sending them tumbling. Lina grappled for control, managing to right the *Star Herald*'s course but knowing another shot could finish them.

'We'll head for it anyway,' she said. 'We don't have a choice. Maybe whoever built it can help us somehow.'

'Wait,' Milo said in amazement. 'Is it moving?'

Somehow the entire massive structure was angling towards them, the base rooted in the ground but the higher levels swinging to face them. As it did so, Lina realised it wasn't a tower at all – it wasn't even straight. The structure curved in the middle like a tall stem weighed down by a heavy, bulb-like cap.

'That's no building,' Milo said. 'It's another mushroom!'

'Is it . . . pointing at us?' Lina asked, their pursuers momentarily forgotten.

As they watched, a series of pale green folds peeled back along the mushroom's cap and the massive protuberance spread wide like a flower, revealing an opening in the centre.

'It almost looks like . . . no, it can't be,' Milo said.

'Go on,' Lina urged him.

'Well, it sort of looks like a cannon, doesn't it?' Milo asked. 'Like a barrel, with the opening at the top and that massive stalk . . . ' Then it hit him. 'Lina, get us out of here. The stalks, remember? Watch out for the stalks!'

But it was too late. Lina saw a ripple building at the base of the huge fungus, making its way up the stalk, picking up speed. When it reached the open bulb something flew out, a gleaming red sphere as big as a TIE fighter's body, glistening with golden spikes.

Lina grabbed the steering bar with all her might, knowing they didn't stand a chance. The projectile slammed into the *Star Herald*'s starboard side, spines piercing the hull. Alarms wailed and sirens blared, but by then they were already going down, spinning helplessly towards the planet's surface.

CHAPTER 2

SCORCHED EARTH

Governor Tarkin removed one black leather glove and ran his finger along the steel railing of the balcony. His fingertip turned black. He shook his head in disgust, pulling a handkerchief from his pocket and wiping his hands clean before replacing the glove.

Everything about this planet was putrid – the air was damp and fetid, the ever-present clouds were gloomy and oppressive, and it seemed as though everything he owned – his clothes, his boots, his weapons, even his prized corvette starship the *Carrion Spike* – had acquired an added layer of creeping black fungus. For a man who prized cleanliness, it was almost unbearable.

A flare of red light caught his eye and Tarkin peered into the gloom. From his vantage point high on the sloping side of the stone compound he could see out across the trackless mushroom forests of Agaris. It was a sight he had already come to loathe – he despised the huge grey domes and the smaller fungi clustered round them, their lurid markings like splashes of neon paint on a grey wall. But his deepest hatred was reserved for those giant stalks, with their infuriating habit of knocking his TIEs out of the sky with their ugly spiked seedlings. He would have ordered them all hacked down if it wasn't for more pressing problems.

The light flared again. He pulled a pair of macrobinoculars from his jacket. Two TIEs were tracking something – could it be a ship? He gripped the railing, watching keenly. Could this be the answer he'd been seeking? Had rebels been here all along, stealing his men from under his nose?

Or could it be . . . yes. He'd heard the reports from Xala's moon, of the fall of Captain Korda and the flight of the Graf children. Where else would they come but here? He smiled. It was almost too perfect.

He sharpened the focus, trying to make out the craft his fighters were pursuing. But the chase seemed to be over, the TIEs circling like rock vultures around a kill. Were the children dead, then? He hoped not; they would be a valuable tool to make their parents talk. Then again, if the droid was still with them he no would longer need the Grafs, so perhaps it would be cleaner if the children had perished.

The entry buzzer whined and Tarkin

gestured. The shutter slid up to reveal a hulking figure almost too large to fit through the doorway. The KX security droid ducked his head and strode out onto the balcony, massive metal arms swinging at his sides. K-4D8's black carapace had been polished to a fine sheen. On one shoulder the Imperial symbol was emblazoned in gold, a symbol of his enhanced status. Seeing this, Tarkin smiled thinly. The droid's loyalties may have been pledged to a man he despised utterly, but all three of them were merely servants to a much greater cause.

'Director Krennic sends his regards,' the droid said, his voice like metal scraping on metal. 'He has commanded me personally to oversee transportation of the first shipment of quadanium back to Sentinel Base. With your permission, Governor.'

'Of course,' Tarkin said softly, pursing his lips. 'And those were Krennic's only orders, were they? Because a more suspicious man might suspect that you were sent to spy on me.'

K-4D8 pulled himself upright, servos whirring. 'My assignment was clear,' he said. 'To escort the first shipment as soon as the ore was prepared. And in the meantime, to place myself in Governor Tarkin's service and carry out any further assignments as he sees fit.'

'Oh, so you're here to help?' Tarkin asked. 'The Director is too kind.'

'He felt that one more pair of hands might speed things along,' the droid explained.

Tarkin's eyes narrowed. 'Yes, that sounds like him. Very well, droid, there's no sense hiding the truth. You know, and Director Krennic undoubtedly knows, that progress has been more than slow. In fact, our mining operations stalled before they even began.'

He gestured down the sloping face of the compound to the courtyard at the bottom. The stone square was littered with the hulks of mining machines – drilling arms and ore extractors, rock pulverisers and drainage pumps, all of it lying idle, gathering fungus. Load-lifters shifted the equipment from one end of the square to the other, and groups of stormtroopers swarmed back and forth, but even from up here Tarkin could see that they had been ordered to look busy, to make it seem as though something was getting done. He knew better.

'The Director was led to believe Agaris had some of the richest quadanium deposits in the galaxy,' K-4D8 said. 'Isn't this compound itself a former mining colony?'

Tarkin nodded. The Imperial base may have looked from the outside like a single steep stone wall, leaning against the mountainside. But the miners had burrowed deep into the rock beneath them, leaving a complex network of dark, winding tunnels.

'Sadly, the seams here have been tapped out,' he said. 'And finding new drilling sites has proved . . . challenging.'

A stormtrooper survey group were gathering in the courtyard, checking their sidearms and securing their helmets. As they turned to face the mushroom forest the soldiers seemed to draw together, clearly reluctant to leave the safety of the compound. Their commander gestured firmly and the troopers moved off, blasters gripped tightly.

Tarkin could almost smell their fear.

'Is the problem one of equipment?' K-4D8 was asking. 'Do your scanners need recalibrating, or do –'

'The men keep disappearing,' Tarkin admitted abruptly. 'We don't know why, we don't know if someone's taking them or if they're simply . . . getting lost. But sixteen patrols have vanished in the past eight days, a total of one hundred and eleven men.'

K-4D8's surprise was evident in his pale metallic eyes. 'One hundred and eleven,' he repeated.

'The few who return have no clear recollection of what happened,' Tarkin went on. 'Some speak of shapes in the mist, eyeless figures ambushing them in the dark. Which is of course impossible. Agaris is devoid of sentient life – the old mining logs and our own sensors agree on that.'

'You suspect outside interference?' K-4D8 asked.

'I have no idea what to suspect,' Tarkin said. 'This foul planet confounds us at every turn. But all is not lost. I have had a pair of prisoners brought here who know everything there is to know about the world of Agaris. They'll give me the answers I seek, or they'll suffer for it.'

The droid leaned closer. 'I am programmed in over ten thousand different methods of interrogation,' he said coldly. 'Please inform me if I can be of assistance.'

Tarkin waved K-4D8 away. 'That will not be necessary,' he said. Then he smiled. 'Though in fact, I do have a task for you. Moments ago, my fighters brought down a craft attempting to infiltrate Agaris airspace. On board there may be two children and a droid, who could be very useful in getting the answers I seek. Take a small squad. If the children survived, bring them to me. And either way, I want that droid's head.'

'Won't your fighter pilots pick up the survivors?' K-4D8 asked.

'This is important to me,' Tarkin told the droid, 'And right now my men have a habit of vanishing. Whatever's out there, I imagine it would think twice about attacking you. And if you do not return . . . well, then I'll know this is serious.'

The droid saluted briskly. 'I shall report back,' he promised, and strode from the balcony.

Tarkin pulled his comlink from his pocket. 'Send up the prisoners,' he ordered. 'And bring a bottle of the Alderaanian white, with three glasses.'

He leaned on the railing, wondering if that patrol was still out there or if they'd already been taken like the others. He shook his head, frustration building in his gut. He refused to let this accursed planet defeat him.

Perhaps it was time for more extreme measures. His men had cut back the foliage surrounding the compound, but he could still see the wall of thick grey stems out beyond the perimeter. They needed to cut further, drive harder, burn this planet clean kilometre by kilometre.

For a moment the clouds broke and a shaft of gold-tinged sunlight touched the fungus forest, sparkling on those huge domed carapaces and setting the smaller, colourful stalks agleam. For that instant, Tarkin mused, it could almost be considered beautiful.

Then the clouds closed and the gloom descended once more.

Rhyssa and Auric Graf were delivered to him in binders by a pair of stormtroopers. Tarkin ordered their bonds removed, showing his prisoners to a small table in the corner of the balcony where a bottle and three glasses had been placed. He poured the wine himself, settling into an upright chair and eyeing them keenly.

The Grafs' incarceration had not been kind, he noted. Both were considerably thinner than their file pictures, their prison garb hanging loose on their bones. Auric had a blue-black bruise high on his cheek, and another on the back of his hand. Rhyssa, too, bore the scars of resistance, but her eyes flashed with anger as she regarded Tarkin, ignoring the glass he placed in front of her.

'Where are my children?' she asked. 'I want to see them. Now.'

Tarkin sipped his wine calmly. 'You're in no position to make demands,' he said. 'And besides, you already know my terms. You tell me everything you know about this pitiful little backwater world – absolutely everything. If I like what I hear, I'll consider returning your children. If not, there's very little I can do. And I warn you, my patience is growing thin.'

'Damn your patience,' Auric growled, his fists clenched. 'How do we know you have Milo and Lina? They evaded the Empire this long, what's to say they aren't still out there?'

'You don't,' Tarkin admitted. 'You are

my prisoners. And if you ever want to see your children alive again, you'll do as I say.'

'What will you do with the information we give you?' Rhyssa asked. 'If we tell you what we know about Agaris, how much of this world will be left when you're done?'

'We know this is a mining operation,' Auric said, gesturing to the machines in the courtyard below. 'There's only one thing you'd be digging for on this world: quadanium. And there's only one thing you'd be building with it. Weapons, so your vile Empire can ruin more lives, oppress more peaceful people. We won't be a part of that.'

'Then your children will die,' Tarkin said flatly, hiding the anger he was feeling. 'It's that simple.'

Auric sank back, biting his lip. But Rhyssa leaned closer, her pale face filled with defiance. 'We won't doom an entire world to ruin, not on your word. You can threaten our children all you like.'

'What's so special about this world?' Tarkin demanded. 'I look out there and all I see is filth and fungus. I might understand your reluctance if there was any sentient life here . . . but there's nothing.'

He broke off, glancing at Auric. Just for a moment, right as he said the word *sentient,* he thought he had seen the man's eyelid twitch. It was only the faintest flicker, but Tarkin was sure it meant something. He had a sense for these things.

A bead of sweat ran down Auric's face and he brushed it away, reaching for his glass and gulping the wine. And with that, the Governor's suspicion became a certainty.

He felt a tremor of excitement. A new species, hidden and uncharted. New recruits for the Empire – or new slaves for his mines, lowering the cost of this operation by orders of magnitude. All he had to do was find them.

'I'll give you one day to change your minds,' he said. 'Then I promise you, our next conversation will be over the bodies of your children.'

He gestured to the stormtroopers guarding the doorway. 'Get these people out of my sight.'

Rhyssa drew close to Auric as they were marched back to their cell. The binders bit into her wrists and her legs were weak from hunger and exhaustion. But there was still strength inside her; she could feel it. She wasn't broken yet, whatever that foul Tarkin might think.

'I don't believe him,' she hissed to her husband as they walked. 'He's lying, he never had the kids.'

‘What if you’re wrong?’ Auric asked. His cheeks were hollow and she saw fear in his sunken eyes. ‘I won’t risk their lives, Rhyss. Even for –’

‘Neither will I,’ Rhyssa cut him off. ‘It won’t come to that. I know it won’t.’

One of the troopers prodded her in the back with his blaster. ‘Move, scum,’ he said, shoving Rhyssa along the passageway.

The corridors in the compound were narrow and poorly lit, moisture glistening on patches of black fungus and green lichen. They descended a long flight of steps, passing a stone arch that echoed to the sound of footsteps and machinery. Inside, Rhyssa could see a high-ceilinged hangar, with two rows of TIE fighters and a dagger-shaped starship bristling with weaponry. She’d lay bets that was Tarkin’s personal craft; the ship had the same air of steely determination as its owner.

An MSE-6 repair droid skittered past, chattering to itself. Otherwise the hangar looked almost deserted – she could see a pair of troopers on duty by the entrance and another two taking apart a TIE engine, but that was all.

From the hangar to the cell she counted the turns – *the first corridor to the left, then along twenty paces. Two right turns, a left, and another right.* Then the cell door was sliding open to admit them, and they were stepping through into their tiny, black-walled enclosure.

The troopers removed their binders and retreated, closing the door. Auric lowered himself onto their bunk, stuffing a mouldy blanket under his head.

'If we could just see them,' he said. 'If we could just know they were okay, for one second.'

‘They’re okay,’ Rhyssa insisted. ‘I feel it. I believe it.’

‘You’re just telling yourself that,’ Auric said, rolling over, his back to her. ‘You don’t know.’

Rhyssa knelt down beside him. ‘We can’t give in to despair. We can’t let him beat us.’

Auric let out a short, bitter laugh. ‘He’s already beaten us, love.’

Rhyssa reached up and squeezed his shoulder. ‘No,’ she said. ‘He hasn’t. Remember?’

And she gestured to the corner of the cell, into the shadows. There, buried in a tiny crack in the black stone wall, was just the faintest hint of colour.

The mushroom’s flat head was barely the size of Rhyssa’s fingernail, but that was twice the size it had been yesterday. The shade was richer too – a burnished orange deepening to red, like the first

flush of sunrise.

One more day, Tarkin had said. She hoped it'd be enough.

CHAPTER 3

IN THE FOG

'Come on, Crater,' Milo insisted, almost pleading. 'We have to go!'

The droid shook his metal head. 'I'm afraid that is simply not possible, Master Milo. This accursed projectile has skewered me like a bladeback boar.'

The spore had slammed into the *Star Herald*'s side, its gold-tipped spines tearing through the hull. Milo and Lina had been lucky – their seats were on the far side of the cockpit. But one of the spikes had plunged right through CR-8R's torso, pinning him in place. The crash had only made things worse, as the spore's weight brought the ship spiralling to the ground. CR-8R's attachments and appendages were now buried under a ton of crushed metal and oozing fungal matter.

'Those TIEs are coming,' Lina called, shouldering her backpack and peering up through the cracked roof. The fighters had used their lasers to clear a landing site among the building-sized mushrooms, and were now circling closer. 'We really need to get out of here.'

'Go,' CR-8R urged Milo. 'I have no time to cut myself free, and there's no sense in all of us being captured. You have to run.'

'But where?' Milo asked him. 'We're on an uncharted planet in some kind of weird fungus forest, and the Empire are everywhere.'

'You'll be fine,' CR-8R insisted,

squeezing Milo's arm with his free hand. 'Trust yourselves, and trust each other. And don't go eating any funny-looking mushrooms.'

Milo nodded. 'We'll come back for you,' he said. 'I promise.'

Then he tore himself away, clambering up through the collapsed cockpit, using the seat backs to push himself up. Morq followed, scampering up into the light. Lina reached down to pull her brother up, and the three of them perched for a moment on the ship's bruised and flattened nose.

'I wonder,' Milo said, 'if there's any class of starship you couldn't crash, if you really tried?'

Lina punched his arm. 'Watch it.'

The TIEs had landed just beyond a dense clump of mushrooms. Milo could hear the chatter of comms as the pilots approached on foot. But now a third craft was hovering, an armoured dropship with open sides. He could see more troops inside, their blasters drawn.

As the ship descended a tall black droid leaned from the hold, grasping the outer railing with one huge hand. Its head turned, spotting them. The droid held up a transmitter.

'Children,' his voice boomed from the dropship's loudhailers. 'You are safe now. There is no need to worry. Stay with your ship.'

Lina snorted. 'Not likely.'

Milo turned to look over his shoulder. The mushroom forest stretched beyond them, all the way to the distant mountains. But just beyond the ship the ground sloped downward, into a series of hollows dark with shifting grey mist.

'That way looks good,' he said. 'Maybe we can lose them in the fog.'

They slid down the *Star Herald*'s steep side, Morq springing ahead. Milo hit the ground running, making for the cover of the big stalks. The soil was spongy black mulch dotted with mushrooms of every shape and colour, from hair-fine lichens to man-sized growths with spreading umbrella-like heads. But there was no dense foliage, nothing to impede them, and for that he was thankful.

They heard the troopers reaching the ship, the echo of blaster fire as they blew the outer hatch. Suddenly Lina's communicator crackled into life. Milo's heart lifted – CR-8R had used this trick before, back on Xirl. He would patch his aural sensors through to the communicator so they could hear what the troopers were saying. Perhaps the droid could talk his way out of this, Milo thought. Or maybe he'd play dead, and the troopers wouldn't bother with him at all.

'The ship's deserted but we've found a droid,' a man said, and Milo recognised the TIE pilot they'd overheard above Agaris. *'It's trapped in the wreckage. We could cut it out, but it'd take a while.'*

'The Governor only needs the head,' the black droid replied. *'Leave the rest.'*

'No, please, wai–' CR-8R managed – then a shot rang out.

The communicator went dead.

Milo looked at Lina, his heart pounding. She shook her head. 'Worry later,' she said. 'Run now.'

Milo did as he was told, sprinting over the marshy ground. *CR-8R might still be okay,* he told himself. This wasn't the first time he'd lost his head.

They reached the first slope, scrambling down a rocky incline. The gloom deepened, the mist thickening as they descended. Around them all was silent: no animal or bird calls, not even the sound of wind. But perhaps it was a good thing, Milo thought – in the stillness they could hear the troopers behind them, the crackle of comms as they marched in pursuit.

At the bottom of the hollow was a narrow stream, running over and beneath a tumble of moss-slick stones. They turned aside, following the flow of water deeper into the valley. The fog thickened, and soon they could hear a deep rushing sound, growing louder as they went. Milo grabbed Lina's hand and they skidded to a halt on the brink of a stony precipice, water tumbling in the darkness below. Morq crouched, peering over the edge and trembling.

Lina cursed under her breath. 'Now what do we do?' They couldn't double back for fear of the troopers, and across the stream the rocks were heaped haphazardly, a tricky climb.

'We don't have a choice,' Milo said. 'We go over and up, right?'

'But there's no cover,' Lina said, looking up. 'If they see us, they'll blast us.' She leaned over the edge. 'We could jump, I guess. But we don't know what's down there.'

Milo followed her gaze. The base of the falls was lost in the gloom. 'No way,' he said. 'But wait, what about that?'

At the edge of the waterfall a large rock jutted out, and beneath it was a shadowy cave. Milo squinted, trying to peer inside. But then he heard the mutter of voices and the splash of boots behind them, and knew their time was up.

'It's the best we've got,' he told Lina. 'Come on.'

They crossed the stream, dropping on the far side and swinging their legs over the edge. Then they clambered down, ducking beneath the shelf of rock. Not a moment too soon – as they retreated into the darkness they heard voices above them, over the rushing of the water.

'There's no sign of them,' the pilot said, his deep voice immediately recognisable. 'The fog's too thick. Request permission to return to the ship.'

'Negative,' the droid's voice crackled through the comlink. *'The Governor*

wants those children found.'

The pilot sighed, and Milo heard his comlink click. 'Since when does a droid get to give orders?'

'Since he was sent by Director Krennic,' his companion replied. 'I hear Krennic and Tarkin hate each other, and Krennic sent K-4D8 to find out what Tarkin's up to.'

'Krennic sent a *droid* to check on Tarkin?' the pilot asked in amazement. 'That's pretty insulting.'

The footsteps stopped at the edge of the falls, right overhead.

'Those kids are long gone,' the pilot sighed. 'I'm guessing whatever took our men took them too. And it'll get us if we stay out here much longer.'

'You know DZ-372 and DX-491 got taken two days ago?' his companion said with a shiver. 'They'd been with us since the Academy. I always figured there was some kind of creature out here, but now I'm hearing it's a secret rebel cell, picking us off one by one. Which would explain that ship back there.'

Milo looked at Lina in surprise. Could it be? The *Star Herald*'s sensors had found no evidence of technology outside the Imperial compound, but surely rebels would have some way of disguising themselves. For the first time since they crashed, he felt a glimmer of hope.

'Whatever it is, this whole planet gives me the creeps,' the pilot said. 'Let's check round those rocks then head b– *What was that?*'

Milo's head snapped up. The fear in the man's voice had been unmistakeable.

'What?' the second trooper asked. 'I didn't see anything.'

'In the fog,' the pilot said. 'Across the stream. There, I saw it again!'

Milo flinched as a trickle of pebbles rattled down into their little cave. Had the trooper kicked them loose, or was it something else?

'I saw it,' the second trooper said shakily. 'It looked . . . big. Bigger than a man, for sure.'

'And it had more arms,' the pilot replied. 'Or were they legs?'

'I don't want to find out,' his companion said. 'Come on, let's get out of here before– *Hey!* Hey, something's got me!'

Lina grabbed Milo, pulling him back. Morq leapt into his lap, shivering fearfully.

'Get it off me!' the trooper was bellowing. 'Shoot it! *Shoot it!*'

They heard blaster fire, followed by a loud scraping like something being dragged over the stones.

'Where are you?' the pilot cried. 'I can't . . . No. *No!* Stay back! Stay back, I'm armed!'

The blaster fired again, twice, three times. Then there was a scream, a crash and silence.

CHAPTER 4

HUNTED

'We don't have a choice,' Lina insisted. 'We can't stay here; they'll send more men. And there's no sense going back to the *Star Herald*. CR-8R's gone and the ship's finished anyway. We have to keep moving.'

'But where?' Milo asked. 'For a moment I really thought there might be rebels here, people who could help us. But you heard. Whatever took them, it wasn't rebels.'

Lina shook her head. 'No. But we're small. Maybe if we stay quiet it won't come after us.'

‘Maybe,’ Milo said. ‘Or maybe we’ll make a perfect after-dinner snack.’

‘So what do you suggest?’ Lina asked, frustrated. ‘The way I see it, our only choice is to stick to the plan. Make for the Imperial compound and hope we don’t run into anything on the way.’

‘It could take days,’ Milo said. ‘You saw how far those mountains were.’

‘So it takes days,’ Lina said. ‘We’ve got enough food in my pack, and we know exactly where we’re going. We stay low, and we stay quiet.’

Milo sighed. ‘Okay,’ he said. ‘But you can go in front.’

Lina shrugged. ‘Fine. If I was a hungry monster I’d take the one at the back first, so the other didn’t notice he’d gone.’

Milo frowned at her. ‘That’s really, really not funny.’

They scaled the rocks as quietly as they could, leaving the waterfall behind. Morq made himself useful, leaping ahead to show them the best footholds. Lina paused, scratching the little monkey-lizard under the chin. He might annoy her sometimes, but Milo's pet wasn't all bad. Morq clicked his beak happily, then scampered off into the fog.

As they reached the top of the rockfall he returned, clutching something in his beak. It was a tiny creature, grey-black and moving slowly. Milo ordered him to drop it and Morq did so, springing back with his tail waving expectantly.

Lina crouched at her brother's side. The creature was like nothing she'd ever seen, a flat disc the size of her palm, covered with fine, sprouting fur. It seemed to have no arms or legs or even a head, but as they watched it rolled over and began to wriggle away, the fur on its belly rippling in waves.

Milo reached out, touching the

creature lightly. It froze, then began to move sideways at precisely the same pace. 'I know it sounds weird,' Milo whispered in amazement, 'but I think this is another mushroom. One that moves. In fact, I think this planet's entire ecosystem might have evolved from fungus. That's why there's no trees or grass. Just mushrooms and lichen and . . . this.'

Lina looked around. The great wide-

capped growths loomed over them, and through a crack in the canopy she could see one of those cannon-shaped stalks jutting into the grey sky. 'The thing that took the troopers,' she asked. 'Might it be a big one of these?'

Milo shrugged. 'Carnivorous fungi have been recorded on several worlds. They trap and consume microscopic organisms. Maybe this one's evolved to digest larger prey.'

'Great,' Lina sighed. 'We're going to be eaten by a giant mushroom.'

The black creature rippled towards Morq, hesitated, then moved in the opposite direction.

'Hey, it backed off,' Lina said. 'Like it saw him and moved away. But I don't see any eyes.'

'Maybe it uses smell,' Milo suggested. 'Or that fur on its back could be sensitive to heat or moisture.'

'So maybe it's actually a good thing we're both so cold and wet,' Lina smiled. 'Come on, let's keep moving.'

The walk was steady at first, as they trudged out of the valley beneath the cover of the spreading mushrooms. At the summit they found a rocky outcrop and took their bearings. The mountains were just a faint smudge on the horizon, a line of black beneath the descending sun.

'Two days,' Lina said, shielding her eyes. 'Three at the most.'

But before long she was forced to revise that estimate. The next valley turned out to be more of a canyon, sheer-sided and so deep that when Milo kicked a pebble over the edge he counted to five before it hit the bottom. They had no choice but to go around, following the ravine as it wove and narrowed, slowly descending. At last they reached a place where the walls were low enough for them to climb down, but by then they sky had darkened, the sun sinking out of sight.

'We'll camp here,' Lina said as they reached the bottom of the canyon at last. 'We'll have walls on both sides and shelter if it rains.'

'And look, firewood,' Milo said, crossing to the far side. One of the big mushrooms had tumbled into the ravine and become wedged beneath a rock, its cap dry and cracking. 'Well, not wood exactly. But it's carbon-based, I don't see why it shouldn't burn.'

'Is that a good idea?' Lina asked. 'The light could attract that . . . fungus monster.'

'It's more likely to scare it away,' Milo said. 'If it does sense heat and moisture it'll definitely steer clear of fire.'

He broke off several large fragments and stacked them, then Lina used her fusioncutter to set them alight. The mushroom burned brightly, sending a dense black smoke spiralling up through the ravine. But she welcomed the heat on her face and the smell was surprisingly appealing.

'I don't suppose . . . ' she started.

'No,' Milo cut her off. 'Crater said we shouldn't eat anything, and I agree. Loads of mushroom species are poisonous.'

'You're right,' Lina sighed. 'I just wish it didn't smell so much like breakfast.'

She rooted in her pack, pulling out a pair of Imperial ration packs and handing one to Milo. The food was dry and tasteless, but it filled her up. Soon her head was nodding, the heat of the fire and the warmth in her belly making her drowsy. She placed her pack on the floor, lying back and resting her head on it. But then she heard Milo's voice.

'Lina?' he asked, and somehow he sounded a long way away. 'Lina, what's happening?'

She sat up, looking around. The smoke was thicker, billowing towards her in black waves. She coughed, covering her eyes. There was Milo, on the far side of the fire. His eyes were streaming, his face red. Lina felt so heavy . . . all she wanted to do was to lie down.

'Milo!' she called, her voice echoing from the canyon sides. 'What is it?'

He turned towards her, stumbling. For a moment the smoke rolled in, hiding him. Lina rubbed her eyes. Then suddenly Milo was at her side, gripping her arm.

'I saw something,' he said urgently. 'In the dark, I saw something.'

'The creature?' Lina asked, her heart quickening.

'I don't know,' Milo admitted. 'I couldn't see straight. I think this smoke's done something to my eyes. And I feel really tired.'

'Me too,' Lina said. 'Come on, let's get away from the fire.'

Milo nodded, turning. But then he stopped dead, squeezing her hand.

Something was standing in the gloom just ahead of them, motionless and wreathed in smoke. At first Lina couldn't make it out; it was just a deeper black among shifting shadows. Then the smoke cleared and she saw a humanoid shape, with two long legs and a trunk topped with a domed head.

'Hello?' Milo called out. 'Who's there?'

Another shape joined the first, smaller and less distinct. Beside it was another, and another. They drew silently closer, creeping over the rocks like

shadows from a nightmare.

'Stay back,' Lina warned them.

The first figure stepped towards her in the firelight, raising one slender arm. There was something grasped in its hand, or claw, or whatever it was: a brightly coloured mushroom, its red cap fringed with orange, like the first light of sunrise. The dark figure held it out, and for a moment Lina had the absurd notion that it was offering the mushroom to her, the way her father would sometimes bring his wife flowers.

Then the cap exploded in a cloud of crimson gas. Lina looked down, confused. A red haze filled her head and she toppled to the ground.

CHAPTER 5

AGARIANS

'Auric, Rhyssa, wake up!'

The voice was soft and close, and he felt a gentle touch on his arm.

'Auric!' the voice repeated. 'Rhyssa! Awake!'

Milo groaned. Why was someone calling his parents' names? His head was clouded, his memory foggy. But when he opened his eyes things didn't really improve – all he could see were tendrils of grey mist and a high stone ceiling. There was a sound all around him, a rushing drone like a great beast breathing, somewhere in the dark.

Then with a start he remembered.

The smoke in the air, the shapes around the campfire. He reached out and felt Lina beside him, just stirring. 'Milo?' she asked blearily. 'Is Dad here? What's going on?'

'I don't know,' he hissed, sitting upright. 'But we're not alone.'

The dark figures stood in a circle around them, silent and watchful. Or at least, as watchful as any creatures without eyes could be. That was the first thing Milo noticed about them – they had heads, or at least places where their tube-like bodies bulged at the top, often tipped by a fringed, toadstool-like cap. They even had mouths, dark slits beneath the cap's brim. But he could detect nothing on these creatures that might be used for seeing.

The walls of the cave were dotted with patches of luminescent fungus, and as his own eyes adjusted Milo could study the creatures more closely. The differences between them seemed greater than the similarities – they all had a roughly cylindrical body with limbs sprouting from it, but that was as far as it went. Some were humanoid, with two limbs below and two above. But others seemed to have three legs and no arms, or six legs like an insect, or no legs and eight tiny arms arranged in a circle. One particularly large specimen close to Milo

had four arms sprouting from the top of its head, and in place of legs a single, twitching tentacle.

Then one stepped forward, and Milo recognised the man-like figure who had approached them the night before. He crouched before them, his skin a pale, silvery grey.

'Auric and Rhyssa,' he said, his soft voice rising above the hissing in the air. 'It is good to have you back on Agaris.'

Lina sat up. 'W– Why do you keep calling us that?' she asked.

The creature seemed confused. 'But that is what you told us to call you. Do you not remember? You told us many things on your last visit, and I cannot recall them all. But your names I could never forget, Auric and Rhyssa Graf!'

His mouth twitched, and to his surprise Milo found himself smiling back. Here they were, stuck in a dark cave surrounded by the strangest bunch of freaks he'd ever seen, and somehow this creature's voice and manner made him feel . . . not safe, exactly, but certainly not as terrified as he had been.

'Auric and Rhyssa are our parents,' he said. 'Do we really look that much like them?'

The creature sat back. 'Parents?' he wondered. 'So you are children.' He looked back at his companions, who all nodded and snuffled to one another. 'That explains a great deal. We were wondering how you had become so much smaller and brighter.'

'Brighter?' Lina asked.

'How to explain?' the creature mused. 'Ah yes. We Agarians – that was the name Auric and Rhyssa gave us, you understand. Agarians. A good name. We Agarians do not have eyes as you humans do. It is strange for us to even imagine it. After long discussions with your mother I had almost come to understand the concept of sight, but now I find it has slipped away again.

'So, we cannot see, but we can sense the world. We smell and we hear. We feel the movement of air and the warmth you emit. And we feel the . . . what was the word Auric used? The vibrations, yes, the vibrations given off by all things. In this way do we see. So when we find a pair of creatures who smell and feel like Auric and Rhyssa Graf, just a little smaller and more vivid with energy, we assume that they have simply changed their form, the way we sometimes do.'

'We can't change our form,' Milo said. 'We're just kids. I'm Milo, and this is Lina.'

He held out his hand and the Agarian did the same, extending a flat, flipper-like paw coated with rows of tiny fronds, all squashy and damp against Milo's palm. Suddenly, he realised.

'You're a mushroom,' he said in amazement. 'All of you – you're living mushrooms!'

The Agarian laughed, a thin wheezing sound. 'In a manner of speaking,' he said. 'You humans have animal ancestors. We evolved, as you say, from fungi. My name is –' And he made a sort of damp purring noise, like Morq sometimes did when Milo scratched his chin.

With a start, Milo remembered his pet. But there he was, stretched out on the stone floor with his legs kicking in sleep. It made sense – if the Agarians had used some sort of gas to knock them out, it'd take longer for little Morq to sleep it off.

Lina tried to pronounce the Agarian's name, but all that came out was a wet huffing noise.

'Hhhuuhhhfffffffrrrrrrr,' Milo managed, and the creature nodded, impressed.

'Good, Milo,' he said. 'Now just a little more swiftly. *Hffrr.*'

'Hffrr,' Milo said. 'I like it.'

Lina was still struggling, a look of frustration on her face.

'It was the same for your parents,' Hffrr smiled. 'Your mother became quite familiar with our speech in the time they were here, but your father decided it was easier to teach me yours. Which is good for us now, is it not?'

'When did they visit?' Milo asked. 'It must have been a long time ago, before we were even born.'

Hffrr seemed to shrug. 'To me, it seems but a moment,' he said. 'But we Agarians measure time very differently. Tell me, Milo and Lina, where are your parents now? It would please me greatly to speak with them.'

Lina's face darkened. 'They're prisoners. Of the Empire.'

Hffrr bowed his head. 'Ah, this is a pity,' he said. 'To think of Auric and Rhyssa, so full of life and teachings, being held by those burning, destroying, metal-hearted –' he made a bitter, spitting noise that Milo could tell was an Agarian curse.

'We came to get them out,' Milo explained. 'But then we crashed.'

'Tell me,' Hffrr said. 'I do not understand everything about your people but . . . are human children not helpless creatures who must be protected by their parents? How is it you have come so far, all alone?'

Milo and Lina looked at one another and shrugged.

'You are no ordinary children, it seems,' said Hffrr thoughtfully.

'We know where they are,' Lina told him. 'They're being held in the Imperial compound. But we don't know how to get to them. Do you know a way in, can you help us get to them?'

'No,' Hffrr said flatly. 'It is impossible.'

Lina's face flushed. 'I know the Empire have weapons – perhaps you are afraid to face them but –'

'We are not afraid,' Hffrr said. 'But we cannot take you to the compound. There is an energy source deep inside that place. It was installed by the miners, and it is the only reason we did not drive them away as we should have done, before their discovery of quadanium brought the Empire. This generator powers the compound, the drills, the lights, the cooling systems, everything. We cannot go near it.'

'But why?' Lina asked. 'What's so terrible about it?'

‘To even come close to the compound means sickness. The energy vibrations are so strong that our senses become confused; it brings on a kind of madness. There is no way to fight it. It is as though the very air itself is our enemy.’ Hffrr shook his head. ‘It is a problem, because our own efforts to fight the Empire have left us in a difficult position. This cave is getting too full.’

He held up one arm and a jet of green gas rushed from his wrist, billowing out into the cavern. Everywhere it went the fog cleared, breaking up into fine droplets that clung to the walls of the cave. Seams of green lichen were revealed, lighting the place with a ghostly glow.

As the mist dissipated Milo could make out other shapes, strewn haphazardly in the base of the cave. He could see an arm here, a boot there. A white torso, a moulded helmet.

Stormtroopers! But all of them were motionless, sprawled on the banks of creeping moss that covered the floor of the cavern. He heard that rushing sound again, and realised it was the sound of a hundred men breathing in unison, hissing and droning in sleep.

'We keep them here,' Hffrr explained. 'We do not know what else to do.'

Milo saw one of the shapes stirring and peered closer. A tiny grey tendril

snaked under the trooper's helmet.

'We keep them fed,' Hffrr said. 'But we cannot return them, they would be back on patrol the next day. Still, we cannot hold them forever. It was our hope that losing so many soldiers might frighten these Imperials away, convince them that Agaris is not worth the effort.'

Lina snorted. 'You clearly don't have much experience with the Empire.'

Hffrr shook his head. 'They are new to us. But we have dealt with invaders before, and survived.'

'Others have come here?' Milo asked, yawning. The effects of the gas had still not completely worn off.

'It is a long story,' Hffrr said, 'and forgive me, but you both seem very tired. You should sleep. Tomorrow I will take you as close as I can to the Imperial compound, and perhaps you will be able to find a way inside.'

'It's a long walk,' Milo said. 'How many days will it take?'

'I know a swifter route,' the Agarian promised. 'I think you will like it. But for now, sleep.'

He showed them to an alcove in the wall, layered with a thick bed of moss. Milo climbed inside, stifling another yawn. Lina turned back.

'If we did find a way in,' she said. 'If we switched that generator off, you could help us find our parents, couldn't you? You'd have no reason to fear the compound.'

Hffrr nodded. 'It might be possible,' he agreed. 'Though many of my people would be against it. We have always tried to avoid violence.'

'I understand,' Lina said. 'But if you want to save your world, you might not have a choice.'

CHAPTER 6

THE SPORE

When they awoke a pale light was filtering into the cavern through fine cracks in the rocky ceiling. The captive stormtroopers lay beneath a layer of mist, their only sign of life that constant breathy roar. Lina sat up beside Milo, rubbing her eyes with one grubby hand.

'Wow,' she said, blearily. 'So it wasn't a dream.'

Milo smiled. 'Afraid not.'

'But we're okay. Aren't we?'

'Definitely,' Milo agreed. 'And we'll see Mum and Dad today. I know it.'

As he sat on the edge of the alcove a tiny shape came bounding from the gloom, leaping into his lap. Morq was bright-eyed and wide awake, waving his scaly tail and nuzzling his beak affectionately against Milo's belly. He stroked the little monkey-lizard's head, feeding him scraps from his ration pack. Morq coughed and spat them out again.

Hffrr appeared soon after, striding through the cave. Milo couldn't help noticing that the Agarian's legs were longer than they had been the night before, his head just a little more human-like.

'Come Milo, come Lina,' Hffrr said brightly. 'We have far to travel.'

He led them on winding paths through the caves, passing from halls the size of hangar bays into tiny, burrowing tunnels where even Milo was forced to duck. The underground system was thronged with Agarians of all shapes and sizes – he saw bulging bodies like great grey Hutts, using arms and tentacles to drag themselves along. But others barely reached Milo's knee, hurrying through the tunnels in little chattering packs. At first he thought they were children, until Hffrr led them past a nursery cave where tiny, grey-capped Agarians came sprouting from the soil, babbling and laughing merrily.

'This is all one system, isn't it?' Milo asked. 'Your people, the big stalks, the

flat mushrooms on the surface, even the moss in the cave. It's all connected.'

'It is the same on any world,' Hffrr agreed. 'Every planet is a sealed system, every part depends on every other part. But you are right, on Agaris the connections are . . . closer.' He tilted his head, gesturing beneath the cap-like brim, and Milo saw tiny coloured fungi clinging to the grey skin. Looking down he saw others on Hffrr's back, and patches of fungus covering his trunk and legs.

'They feed on you?' Milo asked.

'They are part of me,' Hffrr told him. 'These ones resonate on different frequencies and enable me to hear a whole range of sounds. The moss on my back cools me and keeps me from drying out. In exchange I enable them to reach sunlight, to collect nutrients from the air as I move.'

'You can change shape as well, can't you?' Milo asked.

'Yes,' Hffrr admitted. 'Our basic form remains the same – one body, one what you would call "head" – but we can alter our size and the number of our limbs.'

'You changed in the night,' Lina said. 'You look more like a person now.'

'That is true,' Hffrr said. 'Where we are going, I need you to trust me.'

They climbed through a last, sloping tunnel and emerged onto the side of a steep hill surrounded by branching stalks. The sun was up, but Milo couldn't see it through the clouds. Lina covered her eyes, gazing off towards the distant mountains.

'I thought you were taking us to the compound,' she said suspiciously. 'But I think we're further away. Look, there's our ship.' She pointed to a thin trail of smoke on the horizon.

'I said we were going to the compound,' Hffrr agreed. 'I did not say we would walk there. Come.'

He led them to the crest of the hill, where the mushroom forest broke into a stony clearing. In the centre stood a vast cylindrical shape, reaching to the sky. Milo recognised it right away.

'That's the thing that knocked us out of the sky,' he said. 'It nearly killed us!'

Hffrr nodded. 'That was unfortunate,' he said. 'The stalks have an . . . instinct of their own, and love to take shots at Imperial ships. How were they to know?'

Milo peered up at the vast bulb-like protrusion overhead, almost lost in the clouds. The stalk bowed under its weight, the sinewy roots dug deep into the rocks. Hffrr crossed towards it, laying both palms flat. Beneath his fingerless hands the stalk rippled gently, responding to his touch. Hffrr stepped back as a section of it peeled back, folding outward to reveal a dark passageway.

He beckoned. 'This way.'

'Uh-uh,' Lina said, standing firm. 'No way I'm going in there.'

'You must,' Hffrr insisted. 'The only other way is to walk for three days. We do not know what may happen to Auric and Rhyssa in that time.'

'He's right, sis,' Milo said. 'We don't really have a choice.'

He ducked through the opening. The walls inside were cold and clammy, but he could feel life pulsing within. Morq jumped up to crouch on Milo's shoulder, shivering nervously.

Suddenly the walls were gone and he was standing in an open space enclosed by smooth red skin. The chamber was twice Milo's height and seemed to be perfectly spherical. From the base of the sphere sprouted a golden cylinder topped with unevenly shaped branches. Hffrr gestured to it.

'Take hold of the core, Milo,' he said. 'And you too, Lina. Hang on tight.'

'Why?' Lina asked worriedly, following them in. 'What will happen?'

Milo looked up at the ceiling, and gulped. 'I think we're . . . ' he managed. 'I think we're inside . . . '

'No,' Lina said, turning. 'No, we can't . . . ' But the entrance had already sealed up behind them, the walls of the sphere closing seamlessly.

Milo perched on one of the branches, wrapping his arms around the central structure. It was soft but solid in his grip, and the branch beneath him felt equally secure. But still he felt fear in his throat as the sphere began to rise, slowly at first then with increasing speed. It was like being in a turbolift, he thought, only here there were no controls to make it stop, and no upper level. Up they went, faster and faster, until Lina let out a scream and Morq joined her, squawking in terror as they shot up through the stem.

Then there was a loud popping sound, and they were flying free. The wind roared and the walls around them turned a paler red. The spore rocketed upward in a great smooth arc.

'Can you control it?' Lina yelled to Hffrr. 'Or do we just hope for the best?'

Hffrr took hold of the central branch, sliding his palms over the surface. Milo felt the sphere shifting subtly, its direction altering.

'How does it work?' Lina asked.

'Minute flaps in the outer skin,' Hffrr explained. 'They open or close, directing the flow of air.'

'How do you see where we're going?' Milo wondered. 'Or don't I want to know?'

Hffrr smiled, and Milo felt a lurch

as they reached the top of the arc. For a moment they were weightless, clinging to the branching structure. Then there was a cracking, ripping sound and the chamber was flooded with light.

Milo let out a cry as the walls of the spore peeled away, whipping off in the wind that tore at their hair and clothes. Something spiralled from the centre: a long tendril that snapped in the breeze. But as it lengthened it began to unravel, widening to form a flat, almost cloth-like sail. The tether snapped taut and the spore began to descend.

Milo felt his heart thundering, wrapping his arms around the core and trying not to look down. The clouds were far below them, the sun a blazing disc above the curve of the planet.

Lina laughed, her cheeks flushed, her eyes streaming. She reached for Milo's hand, grabbing it tight. He tried to smile back but his stomach rolled, his head spinning. Morq crept inside Milo's jacket, shivering against his chest. He gritted his teeth and clung on.

'There,' Hffrr said, pointing. Towards the horizon, the mountain peaks broke through the clouds like a line of jagged teeth. The sail shifted and they drifted down, buffeted by air currents.

'Can I try?' Lina asked, placing her

hands on the core.

Hffrr nodded. 'Be gentle. You will feel it respond.'

The sail jerked and the spore juddered.

'Are you sure that's a good idea?' Milo asked.

'Don't be daft,' Lina said defensively. 'I can fly anything.'

'You can *crash* anything,' he muttered.

They were descending quickly now, the clouds rushing up to swallow them. For a long time they could see nothing, just swirling grey. Milo shivered, feeling condensation gather on his skin. Then they broke through and the surface of Agaris was revealed.

'I see it,' Lina said, pointing. 'Look!'

Milo followed her finger. There on the side of the nearest mountain he saw the outline of the Imperial compound, a sloping stone structure topped with antenna spikes and gun turrets. At its base was a courtyard filled with the dark shapes of men and machinery.

Hffrr let out a cry, wrapping his hands around the central stalk. 'What is it?' Lina asked.

Hffrr gestured. At the base of the compound the forest had been cleared, cut back for several klicks in every direction. Milo could see troopers on the perimeter, smoke rising as they blasted the undergrowth.

The parachute twisted and the spore began to bank, but their turn was too shallow. Hffrr clutched his head in pain. 'We are too close,' he said. 'I was careless, I brought us in too close. I thought we could take cover in the forest, I did not know they had managed to cut so far.'

In the clearing ahead Milo could see the scorched shapes of giant mushrooms, being dragged away by

Imperial machinery. 'We have to jump,' Hffrr said. 'They will catch us.'

Lina looked down. 'We're not all squashy like you,' she said. 'We've got bones and they break.'

Hffrr clutched his head in agony. 'We are too close,' he repeated. 'I cannot . . . the pain, it is too much. I cannot . . . '

Lina grabbed his hand. 'Go,' she said. 'We'll find a way inside and we'll shut that generator down. Then you can come and rescue us. Okay?'

Hffrr nodded. 'I am sorry.'

Then he let go, toppling backward. Milo saw him plummet to the ground, turning as he fell. He landed spreadeagled on a broad mushroom cap and vanished into the undergrowth.

Milo looked up. The spore drifted slowly down, bringing them closer to the clearing, to the compound, and to capture.

CHAPTER 7

THE PLAN

Rhyssa stared in horror at the head on the desk. There was no light in those metallic eyes.

'Crater,' she said, clutching Auric's arm. 'No.'

Tarkin smiled thinly. 'You asked for proof. Here it is.'

Auric drew himself up. 'And the children?'

'They are safe,' Tarkin said. 'And they will stay that way. You, on the other hand . . .'

Rhyssa nodded. 'Everything you needed was inside Crater's head.'

'Precisely,' Tarkin said. 'The maps

of Wild Space, all your notes on your previous trip to Agaris. I'll admit, it made for fascinating reading. These Agarians, I can scarcely believe they exist. Sentient fungus. They'll have to be wiped out, of course. Unless they could be put to work in our mines.'

'Never,' Auric told him. 'They're too proud.'

Tarkin nodded. 'As I suspected. Ah well, it cannot be helped. They will work, or they will die.'

He lifted CR-8R's head, turning it in his hands. Then he crossed the room, opening a hatch in the wall and dropping it inside. Rhyssa heard a descending rattle as CR-8R's head vanished into the garbage chute.

'Take us to our children,' she pleaded, taking a step towards Tarkin. 'There's no reason for you to keep them from us now.'

He did not turn around. 'It's quite impossible,' he said. 'If you had agreed to my terms, if you had told me what I wanted to know, then perhaps . . . But there must be penalties for defying the Empire, surely you understand that. You will never see your children again.'

He gestured and a pair of uniformed officers strode into the room, laying their hands on Auric and Rhyssa. They tried to struggle but the men were too strong, hauling them back towards the door.

'Please,' Auric cried. 'Whatever you're going to do, just let us see them.'

'No,' Tarkin replied flatly, and the door hissed shut.

They were shoved along the corridor and down the steps. It was all over, Rhyssa knew. She wondered if Tarkin would come in person to see them executed. Somehow, she doubted it.

She reached inside her jacket, her fingers wrapping around the stalk hidden there. They reached the base of the steps, passing the hangar doorway. The whine of machinery echoed within, and she heard the sound of voices.

Then they were past, moving through the poorly-lit corridor. The officer behind Rhyssa gave a shove and she staggered forward. This was it, her best chance.

In a single motion she turned,

drawing the stalk from her jacket and pointing it at the two startled officers. The cap was as wide as her palm now, gleaming blood-red.

The guards stopped abruptly, blasters drawn. Auric had halted, looking at her fearfully.

The officers looked down at the mushroom in her hand. One of them gave a snort.

'Look, she's got a mushroom,' he said, grinning.

'I'm so scared,' his companion chuckled, gesturing with his blaster. 'Enough jokes. Move.'

Rhyssa covered her face with her sleeve as the cap exploded, letting out a burst of crimson gas. The officers were still laughing when they hit the floor, grins pasted on their unconscious faces.

Rhyssa reached down, grabbing their blasters and handing one to Auric. He took it, glaring at her over his sleeve. 'You could've warned me you were going to do that.'

'It was our best chance,' she said. 'If we'd gone back to that cell we'd never have come out alive.'

'So what do we do now?' Auric asked as the red gas dissipated. 'They've got Milo and Lina, remember? We can't just leave them here.'

Rhyssa shook her head. 'I still don't believe it. He'd have let us see them, he wouldn't have been able to resist the chance to gloat.'

'But what about Crater?' Auric protested. 'How could they find him without getting Milo and Lina?'

'I can think of a thousand ways,' Rhyssa said. 'They might've been split up. Crater could've sacrificed himself to save them. And even if they were here we'd have no way to find them. This compound is huge. We need help.'

'The Agarians,' Auric realised. 'You want to go to Hffrr.'

'We have to warn him,' Rhyssa said. 'The Empire know about his people now – they're coming after them.'

Auric pursed his lips. 'Okay,' he said. 'So what's your plan?'

Rhyssa frowned awkwardly. 'This was as far as I got,' she admitted. 'From here we'll just have to improvise.'

They crept back to the hangar, peering through the arched doorway. Rhyssa counted five stormtroopers and three uniformed officers inside, plus a tall black droid who seemed to be giving orders. She gestured to a stack of crates by the doorway and they slipped behind it, keeping low.

'We've searched the area thoroughly,' one of the troopers was saying. 'If there were any rebels on that ship they're gone, along with twelve of my men.'

'Very well,' the black droid replied. 'I will inform the Governor. Rejoin your units.'

He marched towards the door and Rhyssa ducked, her heart thumping.

An alarm blared suddenly, cutting through the din. The droid froze, turning. Then it unslung a large assault rifle from its back and began to stride towards the mouth of the hangar, where the huge cavern opened onto the stone courtyard beyond.

'With me,' the droid ordered, and Rhyssa saw men hurrying to obey, following the tall black figure out into the daylight.

'Well that's convenient,' she whispered, getting to her feet. 'Come on – while they're distracted.'

They hurried towards the nearest TIE. Above them the hatch was raised, a ladder extending down from the fighter's spherical body.

'Can you even fly one of these?' Auric asked as Rhyssa began to climb.

'I can fly anything,' she told him over her shoulder.

Auric shook his head and started up. From the courtyard he could hear shouts and footsteps. Whatever was going on out there, he was thankful for it.

Then another sound caught his ear, and he froze. It was a high-pitched, chattering cry, clearly animal in nature, and strangely familiar. For a moment he was confused. There were no monkey-lizards on Agaris. Why would the Empire have brought one with them?

A tiny shape came hurtling into view, skittering over the smooth stone floor of the hangar. A pair of troopers sprinted after it, blasting indiscriminately. The monkey-lizard ducked behind an open container, looking around in terror. Then it lifted its head, sniffing the air, and looked directly at Auric.

The creature sprang from hiding, scampering madly towards them. 'No,' Auric whispered, waving desperately. 'Morq, no.'

But it was too late. The troopers saw them and raised their blasters. 'Hey,' one of them barked. 'Get down from there!'

Auric looked up, seeing Rhyssa at the top of the ladder. But she wasn't looking at him, or at Morq, or even at the troopers. She was staring out into the courtyard, where a gaggle of figures came striding towards them, led by the black droid. Auric could see four stormtroopers and three green-clad officers. And there in the centre were a pair of prisoners, their heads hanging, their hands bound.

'Lina!' Rhyssa cried, her voice ringing

from the rocky ceiling high above. 'Milo! We're here!'

The prisoners raised their heads, and Auric almost dropped from the ladder in shock.

In the hours that followed, Lina could barely recall how she broke free of the men surrounding them. All she remembered were the shouts behind her, and the sight of her father's face as she sprinted towards him across the hangar. And the joy in her heart, that most of all.

Auric dropped from the ladder, pulling his daughter close in disbelief. Rhyssa clambered down as Milo joined them, weeping as he buried himself in his mother's embrace. Auric spread his arms, enclosing them. They huddled together, sobbing and laughing, ignoring the big black droid as it told them to stand back, line up, obey orders. For that

brief moment, the Empire was a million light years away.

Then Lina heard the men snap to attention, and the air around them seemed to grow colder. Auric disentangled himself, keeping one hand on his son's shoulder as he turned to face the trim, grey-haired figure marching towards them. Lina and Milo wiped their eyes, their hands still locked together.

'Well, isn't this touching,' the man said, regarding them with slate-grey eyes. 'The family Graf, reunited at last.'

Rhyssa pulled her children close. 'You never had them, Tarkin,' she said. 'You were lying all along.'

The Governor tilted his head. 'True,' he admitted. 'But none of that matters now, does it? And finally, you understand. You cannot escape the grip of the Empire.'

'We already have. Like, four times,' Lina said, thrusting out her chin. 'Once more shouldn't be too hard.'

Tarkin looked down in disgust, as though he'd seen something foul on his boot. 'You're no longer dealing with a rank incompetent like Captain Korda. And you have no rebel friends to help you this time. Yes, I know where you have been hiding. And you're going to tell me everything you know, the name of every rebel spy and the location of every safe house.'

'Forget it,' Lina said, ignoring her father's warning hand on her arm. 'We're saying nothing.'

'We shall see,' Tarkin snapped. 'You're lucky you arrived when you did. Each of your parents still has both their eyes, and both their arms. Their hearts continue to beat. It doesn't have to be that way.' He smiled thinly. 'Rest tonight. Tomorrow you will tell me everything.'

And he strode away, followed by the black droid. Lina felt her hands shake as one of the troopers took her wrists, locking them behind her back.

'This way,' he barked, and she was shoved forward. But even as they dragged her away, even as she was driven out into the low, dark corridor, still she felt like she was floating on air.

She glanced back and saw her parents

following, a stormtrooper gesturing with his blasters. Milo walked a few steps ahead, driven by a big trooper with a stun stick clipped to his belt. But when he caught Lina's eye, a grin spread across his features. They'd been through so much. They'd been chased and caught, imprisoned and beaten, shot at and blasted from the sky, and they'd come through all of it. They were still in one piece, and they had achieved what they set out to do.

'Wipe that smirk off your face,' the trooper growled, 'or I'll wipe it off for you.'

But however hard she tried, Lina couldn't stop smiling.

CHAPTER 8

MEAT AND METAL

The smell was driving him wild. It had to be coming from behind one of these doors. But which one? Every time he tried to peek inside the steel would slide shut in his face, or a human in huge boots would barge out and almost step on him. One had even spotted him and given chase, but he had managed to scramble up a rocky wall and hide in a tiny tunnel filled with cold air and echoes.

He didn't know where they'd gone, his boy and his girl. He had vague memories of men in white shooting fire at him, and a friendly face he remembered from the very distant past. He had fled in panic, diving into the darkness, eager to escape all the noise and the blasting. But now he was lost and hungry and alone.

A door at the end of the hallway slid open, emitting a blast of steam. Morq began to salivate – the smell was so strong, it must be the place. He crept closer, alert for any sign of the white men and their big boots. He hunched in the shadows, waiting, and the moment the door moved, so did he.

Morq darted inside, dodging feet, scrambling under a low counter. The room was big and hot and bright, but there appeared to be only one man inside it – a big one with stains on his coat. He was stirring something in a pan, something rich and meaty.

Morq shook his head. Hunger was making him dizzy. He couldn't risk going near the man, but he had to get to the food. He darted from one shadow to the next, freezing at the first sign of movement. Then he realised – it was no use being down here. Humans never put their food on the floor unless they were giving it to you. He had to climb higher.

He scaled a rack of shelves, using his claws to drag himself up. Then it was just a case of jumping across to the counter, a short, easy leap. The surface was smooth and slippery so his landing was far from graceful. But there was his reward – a platter of freshly cut meat, just waiting for him.

Morq looked around cautiously. The big man was still stirring, his back turned.

Morq shot forward, grabbing a slice of meat and scoffing it down. The taste was almost too much – after the dry rations this was a luxury beyond imagination. He gobbled another piece, and another.

He was going for a fourth when a hand grabbed his tail. Morq twisted around, cursing his own foolishness.

The big man had hold of him with one huge fist. And now the other was coming down, a sharp knife glinting as it swung towards Morq's head. He let out a squawk and turned, sinking his beak into the man's hand. The man roared furiously, and the cleaver thudded into the counter top.

Morq yanked free, leaping from the counter and bolting towards the door. But then, disaster – there was someone in the doorway, striding through with a stack of metal trays. The newcomer saw him and yelled, dropping the trays with a crash and a clatter. Morq doubled back, looking desperately for another way out. There, up on the wall, stood an open hatch. It would be quite a leap, but he might just make it.

He crouched, ready to spring. On one side the big man came striding in, his butcher knife raised. On the other the newcomer raced towards him, hands outstretched. Morq jumped, kicking as hard as he could with his legs.

He hit the wall, scrabbling desperately with his claws. For a moment he thought he'd missed his shot, that he was going to fall to the floor and be chopped to bits. Then he felt his long claw catch, the muscles in his arm tightening as he scrambled up and over and into the hatch.

He fell for a long time, slamming into the sides of the metal shaft before plummeting into something warm and sticky and foul. The smells here were overpowering – rotting food and filth, all coming from the slimy pool into which he'd dropped. But there were dry places around the edge – he spotted a tangled heap of scrap metal and machine parts and paddled towards it, dragging himself out of the pool.

He crouched, surveying his surroundings. His boy was not here, in fact he could see no life at all, not even a nice tasty rat. But something was making a sound: he could hear it echoing from the walls and the low rocky ceiling. It was a familiar sound – not a human sound but one he knew.

It was calling his name. Morq darted round, confused. He could see no people, just a strange domed object with glowing eyes. He moved closer, and that's when he recognised it.

Somehow, the Floating Man's head had become separated from the rest of him – an accident that would have killed Morq, but the Floating Man had survived. He was speaking very insistently, and he seemed to want something – Morq recognised the tone if not the words. Then the Floating Man spoke one syllable that the little monkey-lizard recognised: 'Fetch.'

Morq looked around eagerly. What could the Floating Man possibly want in all this rot and junk? He had no way to explain himself – he was just a head. Morq would just have to work it out on his own.

It would probably be something metal, because the Floating Man was metal. Perhaps he was hungry? No, he never seemed to eat. What else would the Floating Man need? What didn't he have?

Then he saw it. Reaching up from the tangle of scrap, a flat disc with five extended fingers. Morq leapt towards it, locking his beak onto the longest digit.

Behind him he could hear the Floating Man still talking. 'Yes, Morq!' he was saying. 'Good Morq! Good!'

Morq felt a flush of warm pride down in his belly, and set to work.

Milo woke to the sound of voices, looking up to see the black droid looming through the cell doorway. Rhyssa and Auric waited in the corridor under guard, their hands bound. Lina sat up, rubbing her eyes.

'Move,' K-4D8 demanded. 'The Governor wants to see you.'

'And what if we don't want to see

him?' Lina asked.

The droid turned towards Rhyssa, raising his heavy assault rifle. Lina leapt to her feet. 'We're coming,' she said. 'Don't do that. Please.'

Milo ran to his mother's side, unable to hug her because of the binders on his wrists. She bent down, nuzzling the top of his head with her nose. 'Get any sleep?' she whispered.

Milo shook his head. 'Not really. I'm feeling sort of tense for some reason.'

Rhyssa laughed.

'Quiet,' K-4D8 snapped. 'No fraternising.'

They marched along the corridor in pairs, Milo and his mother followed by Lina and Auric, and lastly the two stormtroopers. The tunnel divided and they took the left-hand way, ducking into a clammy corridor with flickering lights in the ceiling.

‘Where are you taking us?’ Auric demanded. ‘This isn’t the way to the Governor’s quarters.’

‘We are not going to his quarters,’ K-4D8 retorted, ducking to avoid a clump of lichen hanging from the rocky ceiling. ‘Filthy planet,’ he muttered. ‘So much . . . life.’

Looking around, Milo saw patches of black fungus on the tunnel walls, similar to the stuff that grew on Hffrr’s back. He wondered where the Agarian was now. Was he out there somewhere, making a plan to rescue them? Or had he fled back to his caves, leaving them to their fate?

He blinked. For the briefest moment he’d thought he saw the fungus moving – a faint ripple catching the light. There was a strange low humming in the air.

K-4D8 halted, turning. The troopers drew their blasters. The sound grew louder, a steady drone throbbing from the walls of the tunnel. Again Milo thought he saw the black fungus writhing, like algae on the surface of the sea.

Then suddenly the noise changed pitch, and he could hear words within it. '*Miiiilllloooooo . . .*' it seemed to say. '*Liiiiiinnnnaaaaaaa . . .*'

They looked at one another in amazement. The droid pushed towards them.

'What is that?' he demanded. 'Who is making those sounds?'

'*We're comiiiiiiiing,*' the voice said, and Milo recognised Hffrr's gentle tones. '*Have nooooo feeeeaaaaaaarrr . . .*'

Lina grinned, clapping her hands together. 'They're coming,' she said. Then she looked up at K-4D8. 'You're in big trouble now.'

That was when the shots rang out.

Milo ducked as blaster bolts exploded

in the tunnel, sparks flying from the stone walls. The troopers returned fire, the roar deafening in the narrow space. K-4D8 raised his assault rifle, squeezing off six shots in quick succession.

Milo looked up, trying to see what they were firing at. The lights had been shot out, but at the far end of the hall he could make out a massive moving shape, ducking its head and striding towards them. The troopers crouched, firing back – blaster bolts struck its monstrous torso and the figure reeled. Then it came on again, the floor shaking as it lumbered through the tunnel.

'Identify yourself,' K-4D8 demanded. 'That's an order.'

'I don't take orders from you,' the shape replied, and Milo's mind reeled. *It couldn't be . . . could it?*

The monstrous figure fired at K-4D8, forcing him to duck. Then it paused, beckoning with one massive fist. 'Mistress Lina,' it said. 'Come quickly. You too, Master Milo. I'll cover you.'

'C-Crater?' Lina asked in amazement, getting to her feet. 'Is that you?'

'It's me,' the huge shape said, impossibly. 'Now run.'

Lina did as she was told, jumping to her feet. The troopers were still firing, their blasts striking CR-8R's enormous chassis.

K-4D8 roared 'Stop!' and strode forward, reaching for Lina, missing her by a whisker. He took hold of Milo before he could follow, forcing him roughly to the ground. Then he raised his rifle above his head, blasting at the ceiling.

The tunnel collapsed inward, dust and smoke pouring into the narrow space. Milo heard rocks crashing down, saw one of the troopers borne under by the rubble.

'Lina!' Rhyssa cried. But the second stormtrooper was already shoving them back along the tunnel.

K-4D8 followed, holstering his rifle. 'Move, prisoners. The Governor will not wait forever.'

They staggered through the smoke and dust. Milo saw tears on his mother's cheeks.

'Lina's okay,' he whispered. 'She knows what she's doing. She'll be okay.'

Rhyssa gritted her teeth. 'I hope you're right.'

CHAPTER 9

ATTACK

From end to end the courtyard was filled with men, all standing smartly to attention. Stormtroopers stood in straight rows, their blasters clasped to their chests. The officers lined up beside them, motionless in the red light of the rising sun. At their backs, across a wide expanse of stony ground, the mushroom forest lay grey and misty in the morning haze.

'Ah, K-4,' Governor Tarkin said as the black droid marched from the compound, leading Milo and his parents. 'There were reports of firing in the tunnels. I wondered if you ran into trouble.'

'It was nothing,' the droid reported. 'A blaster malfunction. The Graf girl was injured, I had her sent back to her cell with a medical droid.'

Tarkin's eyes narrowed. 'A pity,' he said. 'I would have liked her to be here for this.'

Why had the droid lied, Milo wondered. It must be ashamed to admit its mistake, frightened of the consequences if Tarkin discovered the truth. The realisation that even a gleaming brute like K-4D8 was afraid of something made Milo feel oddly hopeful. These Imperials might seem unstoppable, they might act like the universe belonged to them. But deep down they had the same fears as everyone else.

Tarkin turned to Auric and Rhyssa, gesturing out into the courtyard. 'Impressive, isn't it? I wanted to inspect my troops one last time before we begin.'

'Begin what?' Rhyssa asked through gritted teeth.

'Why, my takeover of Agaris, of course.' Tarkin smiled cruelly. He nodded to one of his men, who hurried forward to remove their binders. 'You know, you made all of this possible, you and your children. The records we found in your droid's head told us everything we needed to know about these Agarians, including how to kill them. My troopers have had new air filters fitted into their helmets, they won't be breathing any more of that filthy gas.'

He gestured up into the sky, where a phalanx of black shapes came screaming through the clouds. Shielding his eyes, Milo saw the familiar twin-pod shapes of TIE bombers.

'They've been fitted with special mining charges,' Tarkin went on. 'Cave crackers, they call them. They'll tear this planet open like a rotten fruit, and my men will mop up the remains. In a matter of days, Agaris will be mine.'

He turned away, raising a comlink to his mouth. The men in the courtyard fell silent. The air was perfectly still; all Milo could hear was the screech of engines as the bombers sped closer. Agaris held its breath.

Governor Tarkin drew himself upright. 'Today –' he began.

Then everything fell apart.

The frontmost TIE bomber let out a roar, black smoke pouring from the starboard pod. It began to spin madly, dropping out of formation. Milo saw a spiked spore jutting from one wing panel.

Tarkin looked up, his face white with fury. The men in the courtyard began to turn, their ranks breaking. Milo saw one of the huge stalks way off in the distance, its barrel-like stem raised.

The bomber tumbled, screeching towards the courtyard. The pilot tried to pull up, but it was no use. The ship slammed into the face of the compound like an insect on a speeder's windshield. Hunks of twisted metal came tumbling down the sloping stones, shattering in the courtyard to either side of them. Troopers and officers alike scrambled back, all order collapsing.

'Hold formation!' K-4D8 barked, his vocabulator at maximum.

Then Milo heard a cry, and he raised his head. Above the grey line of the mushroom forest a line of dark specks was rising. They arced towards the compound, cutting a smooth course. Milo was confused; the red spores would be no use against solid stone. They'd splatter on the compound wall just like that bomber.

But these spores were black, not red. And as they curved towards the courtyard they exploded in mid-air, popping like a row of fireworks. Crimson smoke burst from them, descending in a thick cloud. 'Helmet filters on!' K-4D8 ordered.

But many of the officers and compound staff had no helmets, and as the gas settled Milo saw them slumping to the ground, some laughing and twitching, others just dropping on the stones. One of Tarkin's men approached with a case of breath masks, handing them out hurriedly. The Governor clamped the mask to his face, breathing through the clear plastic air pipe.

'Give them to the prisoners,' he said. 'I want them to witness my response.'

Milo took the offered mask, tying the strap around his head and trying to breathe calmly. The red gas had begun to

dissipate, leaving a trail of unconscious figures spreadeagled on the stones. In the silence he heard cries of pain and confusion, the crackle of comms and men barking orders.

Then another sound rose, faint and distant but impossible to ignore. It came from beyond the courtyard, beyond the expanse of cleared ground. It came from deep within the mushroom forest itself. It was the sound of voices, hundreds of them, raised in anger. Their cry was wordless but the defiance in it was unmistakeable. Milo felt his hopes rise. The Agarians were coming.

A second line of spheres appeared on the horizon, spiralling towards them. They pulsed with a sickly purple light, as though something inside was glowing. Then, like the first set of spores, they exploded in mid-air, sending thousands upon thousands of tiny, glistening pellets raining down upon the men in the courtyard.

Milo ducked, hearing a clanking hiss like hailstones on a tin roof. But when he looked again the stormtroopers were picking themselves up, their armour dented but not pierced by the rain of seedlings.

Tarkin smiled grimly. 'Is that the best these Agarians have got?' he spat. Then he raised his voice. 'K-4, wipe them out!'

The black droid nodded, striding out into the courtyard. The troopers were beginning to reform, their weapons pointed back towards the forest. The droid marched among them, issuing commands. The remaining TIE bombers circled back, and Milo saw gouts of fire blossoming along the line of giant stems, a curtain of orange flame exploding from the fog. He heard distant cries, lifted on the hot wind that tore towards them.

The first line of stormtroopers moved forward, flamethrowers raised. At a signal from K-4D8 they hit their triggers simultaneously, scorching the ground ahead of them. The bombers returned, unleashing another wall of fire. Milo saw huge mushrooms in flames, their caps cracking and crumbling in the inferno. And he saw other shapes too, scrambling clear of the raging firestorm and disappearing into cracks in the ground.

The Agarians were out there, withstanding the Imperial assault. But unless the generator was put out of action they were stuck where they were, unable to close in on the compound. At any moment the first stormtroopers would engage them, and Milo had no idea how that fight would play out. The Agarians were many, but the troopers were better armed, better trained and had no doubts when it came to killing.

He wondered desperately where Lina could be. As far as he could tell, there were two possibilities – either she was lying injured under a rockfall, or she and Crater were on their way to find the generator. For all their sakes, he prayed it was the latter.

CHAPTER 10

THE GENERATOR

'And then I think the fall must have triggered my reactivation response, because when I came to my senses I was in a garbage pile,' CR-8R was saying. 'Truly, Mistress Lina, you can't imagine how I've suffered. It's a miracle that I'm here at all. In one piece, or near enough.'

In one very big piece, Lina thought to herself. She was finding it impossible to come to terms with CR-8R's new body as he stomped alongside, kicking up clouds of dust with every crashing footstep. Lina had seen load-lifters at work; she'd almost been flattened by one in a mining yard on Cedonne. This one was battered and bent, its one remaining arm grasping a bulky blaster. The torso was almost as wide as the tunnel itself, terminating in a pair of massive, tree-trunk legs. Perched off-centre atop this vast cube, CR-8R's head looked like a bolo-ball balanced on a scout walker.

Lina didn't know where the other arm had originated, but she suspected it was from some kind of lumber droid. The long, slender limb terminated in a toothed power-saw that kept starting up at the worst moments, like when Lina had pulled CR-8R in for a hug after the shootout in the tunnel. He'd meant to comfort her, and ended up almost taking her head off.

'It wasn't a miracle that saved you,' she reminded him. 'It was a monkey-lizard.'

'I suppose so,' CR-8R agreed reluctantly. 'This . . . animal proved himself useful after all.'

'And after all the mean things you've said about him,' Lina grinned. 'You should apologise, Crate.'

CR-8R sighed. 'Morq, I am sorry I did not appreciate your worth sooner. Thank you for rescuing me.'

Morq purred, clambering onto CR-8R's massive shoulder and rubbing his beak lovingly against the droid's metal cheek. CR-8R gave a reluctant purr of his own, and Morq sat back happily.

'According to the schematics I accessed in the compound's mainframe,' CR-8R said, 'the generator should be at the end of this hallway.'

'It'll be guarded,' Lina warned. 'They can't all have gone off to this inspection thing.'

The corridors had been mercifully empty, but they had overheard a pair of mechanics bickering over whose fault it was that they were late for the Governor's personnel review.

'I hope Milo's okay,' Lina went on. 'That ceiling came down pretty hard.'

'I'm sure he was clear of the impact zone,' CR-8R told her. 'That KX droid would not risk both of his Governor's prized prisoners. He hasn't had the chance to question you yet.'

'I wouldn't tell him anything anyway,' Lina muttered.

'You'd tell him whatever he wanted to know,' CR-8R said. 'You would not risk your life, or those of Master Milo or your parents simply for some information that might already be out of date.'

'But he wanted to know about Mira and Ephraim,' Lina protested. 'And their whole network.'

'And if the Bridgers were here, they would tell you the same,' CR-8R said.

'They can look after themselves.'

There was a rumbling overhead and the walls shook. The lights in the ceiling flickered, and far away Lina heard a dull, rolling crash. 'It's started,' she said. 'We need to move.' She picked up the pace, hurrying along the tunnel.

'Hey!' A shout froze her in her tracks. 'What do you think you're doing?'

At the end of the corridor a steel door stood wide. A pair of young crewmen huddled in the entranceway, awkwardly clutching blasters.

'Halt!' the nearest one cried. 'Or we'll open fire.'

'Crater,' Lina hissed. 'What are going to do now?'

'Fear not, Mistress Lina,' CR-8R said. 'I have it under control.'

He began to run, his huge feet slamming on the stones. To Lina's amazement he let out a roar, charging down the corridor towards the startled guards. One of them fired, the blast ricocheting off CR-8R's armoured torso. But still he kept coming, Morq clinging to his shoulder and letting out a screech of his own.

The crewmen looked at one another in surprise and terror. They were barely more than cadets, Lina saw, left on guard while their superiors attended the inspection. She could only imagine their terror as they saw that massive shape thundering from the shadows.

The lead crewman broke first, bolting back through the doorway and pulling his companion with him. He slammed the door controls as he fled, but CR-8R reached the door before it could slide shut, grabbing it in his massive fist. The steel tore like paper as the droid charged through.

Lina hurried after him, pushing past

the twisted door and into the generator room. On the far side she saw another panel hissing shut.

'You let them go,' she objected.

CR-8R nodded. 'I may look like a monster, Mistress Lina, but that does mean I have become one.'

The ground shook again, dust drifting down into the room.

'They'll be back,' Lina said. 'And they'll bring reinforcements.'

'Then we should do what we came to do,' CR-8R said. 'And quickly.'

The generator towered over them, a black cylinder shimmering with coloured lights. Lina could feel its power – the air was greasy with electricity and blue sparks danced overhead.

'Do you think there's an off switch?' she asked.

'Perhaps,' CR-8R told her. 'But it could take time to find it. This will be quicker.' And he fired up his power-saw attachment, swinging it down on the console in front of them. Sparks flew, shards of metal and plastic hissing through the air.

Lina ducked. 'Hey, careful,' she protested. 'We're not all covered in armour.'

'My apologies,' CR-8R said. 'Take shelter behind me, Mistress Lina.'

He drove his saw into the centre of the console, the blade whining as the teeth dug in. With the other hand he aimed his blaster, hammering the console with four quick shots.

'Hit it again!' Lina cried. 'I think it's working!'

Steel melted and hissed. The generator juddered, sparks of electricity showering down on the shattered console. Morq ran for cover as electric bolts arced through the air.

Then with a cough and a groan, the generator gave out and they were plunged into darkness.

'Nice work Crate,' Lina said. 'Now all we have to do is find our way out again.'

'I'm afraid my new body does not seem to possess any glowlamps,' CR-8R said apologetically. 'However, I can see by infra-red. I will attempt to locate a light source. Ah, what's this?'

Lina heard a click, followed by a hiss of static. 'That doesn't sound like a torch to me,' she said.

'Very astute,' CR-8R said. 'It's a radio. Perhaps we can get some news of Master Milo, or at least find out what is causing these earthquakes.' He scanned through the Imperial bands. Suddenly a voice leapt from the darkness.

'The creatures are moving towards us,' it crackled. *'I can't . . . I can't quite make them out.'*

Between the words Lina could hear explosions and blaster fire, and troopers barking orders. '*Wait,*' the man went on, his voice trembling. '*The smoke's lifting. I see . . . I see them. They're coming this way. Sir, there are hundreds of them!*'

'*Hold your position!*' a second voice snapped, and Lina recognised K-4D8's cold tones. '*Use flamethrowers and blasters, but hold them back.*'

'*There are too many of them!*' the trooper cried out. '*They're everywhere! They're coming out of the fog! Aieeeee . . . .*'

His scream trailed off, and for a moment there was silence. Then the droid's voice cut back in.

'*Hangar, this is K-4D8,*' he said. '*Prepare the* Carrion Spike *for immediate lift-off. And have the brig prepared: the Governor is taking his prisoners with him.*'

'*Right away,*' a voice responded.

'They're taking them to the hangar,' Lina said. 'Do you know the way?'

'Of course,' CR-8R said, and in the darkness she heard his servos whirring. 'Follow my voice.'

'Right with you, Crate,' Lina called out, holding up her hands. She felt the ragged edge of the busted door and pushed through. In the corridor the air was cooler, but just as dark.

'Reach out to your left, Mistress Lina,' CR-8R said, and Lina did so. She felt something smooth and round, wrapping her hand around it.

'It feels like a pipe,' she said, lifting it. 'What do I need it for?'

'To defend yourself, if need be,' CR-8R replied. 'Between us, we should now be equipped to repel any Imperial attacks.'

Lina laughed.

'What is so amusing?' the droid asked.

'You,' Lina said, hefting the cold steel and feeling a bit braver. 'I remember when you were scared of everything, always telling us to be careful, go slow, don't take any risks. Now you're telling me to take on the Empire with a metal pipe.'

'Maybe this new body has gone to my head,' CR-8R admitted.

'It's not just that,' Lina said. 'It started before we even landed on Agaris. You've gotten tougher, Crate.'

'Perhaps,' CR-8R agreed. 'But so have you, and Master Milo. We have been forced to confront situations that none of us could have imagined before your parents were taken. We have all changed.'

'I guess you're right,' Lina sighed. 'But it's a good thing, right?'

'For the most part,' CR-8R agreed. 'You and Master Milo can take care of yourselves now. If such a disaster should happen again, you would be well equipped to deal with it.'

'But?' Lina asked.

'But you are still so young,' CR-8R said. 'Children your age should not have to fight for their lives. They should not have to make the choices you have been forced to make.'

'I doubt we're the only ones,' Lina pointed out. 'This must be happening all across the Empire. Kids losing their parents and their families, having to struggle like we did.'

'Indeed,' CR-8R said sadly. 'I think of them often.' Then he picked up the pace. 'Come, Mistress Lina. We must be swift. If Governor Tarkin achieves lift-off, this has all been for nothing.'

CHAPTER 11

THE BATTLE

'Move, boy,' K-4D8 barked, shoving Milo forward. He stumbled, grabbing his father's hand. Auric turned, glaring at the droid and the stormtroopers marching behind.

'Knocking my son down won't make us go any faster,' he said angrily.

'He's right,' Tarkin agreed, turning in the tunnel. 'There is no need to be rough. Just know that the faster you move, the faster you'll be safe on my ship.'

'We're not getting on your ship,' Rhyssa spat. 'You'll have to kill us first.'

'As you will,' Tarkin said. He marched ahead, leading them out into the hangar.

The *Carrion Spike* stood on the far side of the cavernous space, gun turrets gleaming. Power droids buzzed around the ship's landing gear, and Milo could see a pair of officers hurrying down the gangway, making their final checks. Inside, all was black.

'Milo, look,' Auric hissed, and he turned to follow his father's gaze.

Out beyond the hangar's open entranceway, all was chaos. The red gas rolled in waves, hiding much of the courtyard from view. But Milo could see enough.

He could see bodies littered on the ground, some motionless, some slowly moving. Most were Imperial officers, the ones who'd gone down when the gas first descended. But he saw a few stormtroopers too, and here and there a large grey shape.

An explosion sounded, waves of heat

driving the red smoke back. As the noise faded Milo saw the front line of the Agarian attack, driving raggedly towards the compound. A misshapen wall of grey, they came rushing and rolling across open ground to the edge of the courtyard. The stormtroopers retreated, attempting to repel the enemy with blasters and flamethrowers. But the Agarians were too many; they overwhelmed the troopers, returning fire with gas-guns and fleshy slings that shot out pods filled with dagger-sharp pellets.

Governor Tarkin watched silently; if he was in any way troubled by what he saw, he refused to show it. 'Get them on board,' he told K-4D8. 'Quickly, now.'

The droid took hold of Milo's shoulder, almost lifting the boy off his feet as he marched towards the waiting ship. The troopers shoved Auric and Rhyssa forward, the officers from the

Carrion Spike crossing the hangar towards them. 'She's prepped and ready, sir.'

'Good,' Tarkin said. 'Secure the prisoners. I will pilot the ship myself.'

Milo heard blaster fire, closer now. He turned as the smoke in the hangar's mouth parted, revealing a group of dark figures.

'Stop,' the closest Agarian demanded. 'Let them go.' Milo knew that voice.

Tarkin turned at the foot of the gangway. The stormtroopers closed ranks, shielding the Governor. K-4D8 froze, holding Milo by the collar.

'Let them go,' Hffrr repeated, his soft voice echoing. 'Now.'

His companions halted. There were seven of them, ranging from a waist-high sproutling to a pair of four-armed monsters half the size of a TIE fighter.

Tarkin peered at the Agarians

with disgust, as though here was the embodiment of all he loathed about this planet. 'These people are my prisoners,' he said. 'They're coming with me.'

Hffrr took a step forward. 'You are in command here?'

'I am the authority on Agaris,' the Governor agreed. 'My name is Tarkin.'

'Taaah-kin,' Hffrr said. 'Yes. Your name is known to us. We have your men.'

The Governor pursed his lips. 'I thought as much. Are they dead?'

'No,' Hffrr said. 'They are simply sleeping. If you leave this planet, they will be returned to you.'

Tarkin gave a dismissive wave. 'If those men were foolish enough to get captured, I have no use for them.'

Hffrr took another step. 'That is your choice,' he said. 'But you will not take these people.'

Tarkin sighed. 'I grow tired of this,' he

said. 'K-4D8! Kill them, would you?'

The black droid nodded once. 'With pleasure,' he said, and opened fire.

One of the Agarians toppled back, green gas erupting from his body. The rest took cover behind a stack of crates as the stormtroopers blasted them. Sparks flew, lighting up the hangar.

'Auric and Rhyssa, take cover,' Hffrr yelled out, and something rolled towards the troopers, a tiny round seedling. The Grafs ducked as the fungus grenade exploded, darts thudding into the stormtroopers' armour and knocking them to the floor. Milo was protected by K-4D8's metal body; the droid barely flinched as three of the darts pierced his black chassis.

The Agarians advanced, Hffrr leading the charge as they ran and rolled towards the shuttle. Tarkin stood for a moment, looking down at his fallen troopers and up at the approaching Agarians. Then he turned and marched up the gangway, raising it behind him.

K-4D8 backed into the hangar, dragging Milo by the collar, his feet scraping on the stones. He kicked, trying to twist free, but K-4D8 barely seemed to notice. Milo saw two troopers staggering to their feet, firing wildly. One of the big Agarians fell, shrouded in green gas.

Rhyssa grabbed the nearest trooper around the waist, relieving him of his blaster. Auric took hold of the other and they wrestled on the stones. Milo saw his father wrap his hands around the trooper's throat.

Then there was a roar and a wave of heat, and the *Carrion Spike* began to rise. Through the cockpit window Milo could make out the back of Tarkin's head, bent over the controls as he piloted the ship out of the hangar. The thrusters roared and the cavern was bathed in light and heat. Then the ship was gone, tearing through the clouds and vanishing into the murky sky.

'Let Milo go,' Hffrr ordered, taking a step towards K-4D8. In his hand he held a blaster, taken from one of the fallen troopers. 'Let him go, and you will live.'

The droid pulled himself upright. Milo crouched at his feet, K-4D8's hand still tight on his collar.

'Stop where you are,' the black droid ordered. 'Stop or I'll kill your precious boy.'

'I will destroy you first.' Hffrr raised the blaster, aiming it at K-4D8's gleaming head. They were the same height, the metal monster and the slender Agarian. 'Release him, or I will use your own weapon to finish you.'

'I don't believe it,' K-4D8 replied. 'You are weak. You will not kill me.'

Hffrr said nothing, his hand

trembling where it held the gun.

'It's a machine,' Rhyssa urged him. 'It's not alive. Take the shot.'

Hffrr glanced at her, confused. 'It speaks,' he said. 'It thinks.'

'It's not the same,' Auric joined his wife. 'Do it. Save Milo.'

Hffrr looked down at the blaster, then up at the droid. Milo could see the conflict on his smooth grey face. Then slowly, he lowered the gun. 'This is a sentient being. I cannot kill it.'

'I, however, do not have that problem.' The voice boomed from the back of the hangar, deep in shadow.

K-4D8 span around, pulling Milo with him. Something was emerging from the darkness. He heard the whine of a power saw.

'Put him down,' CR-8R demanded, striding forward on massive metal legs. 'Now.'

Lina hurried behind him. She saw Milo and froze, one hand on her mouth, the other gripping a rusty piece of pipe.

'You look . . . different,' K-4D8 said, raising his assault rifle.

'I feel different,' CR-8R agreed.

Then he fired and ducked simultaneously, K-4D8's blast missing him by a whisker. The black droid was not so quick; CR-8R's shot struck him in the shoulder, sending sparks flying. His hand snapped open inadvertently, releasing Milo.

K-4D8 let out a roar of frustration, reaching for the boy. But before he could take hold CR-8R came storming in, the power saw raised. He swung it down, the steel teeth grinding into K-4D8's arm. The black droid turned, grabbing CR-8R with one huge metal fist. They wrestled, servos grinding and sparks flying. Their feet slammed into the floor of the hangar,

cracking the stones.

First CR-8R had the advantage, his saw biting deep into K-4D8's exposed shoulder wiring. Then the black droid went low, jamming his rifle into CR-8R's torso and firing twice. CR-8R's armour was solid but the blasts drove him back. He put his head down and charged again, grabbing K-4D8's rifle arm. The next shot went wild, barely missing Lina as she ran to her brother's side.

They took shelter behind the wing of a TIE fighter, watching as the droids grappled furiously. 'What happened to Crater?' Milo asked, amazed.

'Long story,' Lina said. 'It sort of suits him, though, right?'

'I think he's winning,' Milo said. Then he raised his voice. 'Come on, Crater! Rip his arms off!'

'I'm trying, Master Milo,' CR-8R called back, striking a blow that knocked K-4D8 flying. The black droid landed on his back with a crunch.

'Stay down,' CR-8R ordered, marching towards him. 'Or I will crush you. Nobody touches Master Milo and gets away with it.'

K-4D8 pulled himself up. One arm was crooked, sheared cables sparking in the hollow of his shoulder. 'I fight for the Empire,' he said. His vocabulator had been damaged, making his voice sound slow and mean. 'I fight!'

And he lumbered forward, lowering his head. Contact came and CR-8R staggered back. K-4D8 swung wildly, his huge fist pummelling CR-8R again and again in the same weakening spot. To Milo's horror he managed to punch through, and sparks flew as K-4D8 twisted and tore with his fingers. CR-8R let out an electronic whine, falling back with oil gushing from his chest.

'No!' Lina cried out, jumping to her feet. She sprinted from the TIE's shadow, wielding her pipe.

CR-8R struggled on his back like an insect, trying to stand, but the bulky body was too heavy. K-4D8 put a foot on his torso, holding him down. He lowered his assault rifle, pressing it to CR-8R's head. Milo knew that if he destroyed those cranial circuits, there'd be no coming back. CR-8R would be gone forever. He jumped to his feet, following his sister.

'Kids, no!' Auric yelled, and Milo glanced back to see his parents hurrying towards them, hands raised. Hffrr was with them, striding across the hangar.

But Milo and Lina ignored them, running at K-4D8, yelling like animals. Lina swung her pipe, smacking the droid in his articulated back. There was a loud metallic clang. She hit him again and again, whaling as hard as she could. Milo ran in, grabbing K-4D8's gun arm.

The droid growled in frustration. 'Children,' he drawled. 'Foolish.'

'We won't let you touch him,' Milo yelled. 'We won't!'

K-4D8 leaned in until his cruel face was just centimetres from Milo's. 'Kill you first,' he growled. 'Then finish your friend.'

And he raised his gun arm, lifting Milo right off his feet. He clung on, trying to pull the droid down, but he simply wasn't heavy enough. The rifle swung back towards Lina. Dimly Milo could make out something moving on the edge of his vision, something rising from the floor.

Lina took a step back as K-4D8 turned on her. She held the pipe in front of her defiantly, and Milo was reminded of his parents' old bedtime stories about the Jedi and their lightsabers. Lina faced the droid, her face firm, the pipe raised.

K-4D8 laughed and took aim.

There was a screeching metallic whine, and Milo felt hot sparks spraying the side of his face. K-4D8 staggered and Milo dropped, turning to see the tall black droid still upright, an expression of shock on his face. His head began to vibrate, as if it was about to explode. Fragments of steel and plastic erupted from his neck.

Then there was a clunk and a hiss and K-4D8's head slumped forward. It struck his chest and rolled to the floor, landing with a hard metallic thud. The black droid fell to his knees, and Milo jumped back as the decapitated body dropped like a tree.

Behind him CR-8R was revealed, his power saw raised victoriously. Then his knee joints weakened and he, too, staggered, sitting down hard on his armoured backside.

Lina ran to him, wrapping her arms around his head. Morq leapt onto CR-8R's shoulder, licking his face excitedly.

Milo grinned. 'That was without doubt the most awesome thing I have ever seen.'

CR-8R looked up at him. 'I am glad to be of service, as always.'

Rhyssa joined them, looking down at K-4D8's motionless form. 'I don't think I ever programmed you for battle, Crater,' she said.

He nodded weakly. 'You'll find a lot has changed, Miss Rhyssa.'

Auric crossed to join Hffrr. He was gazing out at the courtyard, his arms crossed. The battle was over, and through the drifting smoke Milo could see the Agarians lifting the unconscious officers and lining them up on the stones. The surviving stormtroopers sat in a square, their arms crossed over their heads. The Agarians had collected their blasters, throwing them into a tangled heap beyond the courtyard. As Milo watched the earth cracked open and the weapons toppled into it, vanishing from sight.

'Tarkin will return,' Auric said to Hffrr. 'You know that, right?'

'I do,' Hffrr agreed. 'I saw it in his eyes. He will come back, and he will destroy everything.'

'So what are you going to do?' Auric asked. 'You can't fight him. He'll bomb you from orbit if he has to.'

'It is time for us to leave,' Hffrr said. 'We have suspected this for some time. The preparations are already in place.'

'Leave?' Milo asked, joining them. 'Leave how? You don't have any ships.'

Hffrr smiled at him. 'You will see, young Milo,' he said. 'You will see.'

CHAPTER 12

EVACUATION

Lina buckled into the co-pilot's seat as Auric made a final check of the *Star Herald*'s flight controls. Lights rippled across the freshly soldered console as Milo took his seat behind her, checking the navigation array.

'How we doing back there?' Auric called, and Lina twisted to peer into the darkened hold. She saw a spray of sparks, and heard her mother curse loudly.

'We're almost there,' Rhyssa shouted back. 'Crate, hand me the hydrospanner.'

The Agarians had delivered the ship at sunrise, hauling it through the mushroom forest using ropes and rollers. Rhyssa had set to work right away, patching up the *Star Herald*'s smashed side and refitting the cables that ran from the cockpit to the engine. Thankfully the thrusters were undamaged, and once CR-8R had reconnected with his old chassis he was able to help her make the final repairs.

'This bucket of bolts had better hold together,' Auric muttered, reaching to trigger the fuel feeds.

'She will,' Lina told him. 'She's not bad, for an Imperial ship. She's just had a few knocks.'

'We should've asked to borrow one of those,' her father said, pointing. 'I'd feel safer.'

Through the viewport they could see an Imperial transport lifting off from the compound, soaring up towards the Star Destroyer waiting in orbit. A handful of stormtroopers still huddled in the courtyard, waiting to be evacuated.

'I can't believe Hffrr's just letting them go,' Lina said. 'If they'd kept hold of their prisoners the Agarians would've had something to bargain with.'

'It wouldn't make any difference,' Auric told her as the transport vanished into the clouds. 'Tarkin wouldn't think twice about bombing this planet to smithereens, whether or not his men were still on the surface.'

Lina felt sick. 'That's horrible,' she said. 'He's a monster.'

'He is,' Auric agreed. 'But Hffrr isn't. He'd rather let them go, even though he knows they'll rejoin their units. I admire that.'

Lina nodded. The thought of all those Imperial soldiers getting away free made her furious, but she knew her father was right. If the Agarians left them to die, they were no better than the Empire.

'So what do *you* think's going to happen?' Milo asked, leaning between the seats. 'What did Hffrr mean when he said it was time to leave?'

Auric shrugged. 'Your guess is as good as mine,' he said. 'On our last trip, we never saw any sign that the Agarians had interplanetary technology. But there's so much we don't know about them. I mean, Hffrr looks basically the same as he did thirteen years ago. He hasn't aged.'

The Agarians had been busy all night making preparations, but what it all meant Lina couldn't begin to guess. New growths had sprouted from the mushroom forest, vast bowl-shaped fungi that towered over even the highest stalks. Since dawn there had been no sign of Hffrr or his people; they had delivered the *Star Herald* and retreated underground. She wondered if he would come to say goodbye.

Another Imperial ship landed, wings folding as it touched lightly on the stones of the courtyard. Auric's eyes narrowed. 'That has to be the last one,' he muttered. 'We really need to go. What are they doing back there?'

'I can hear you, you know,' CR-8R called from the hold. 'We are working as fast as we can.'

'I know,' Auric said. 'Work faster.'

'Hey,' Rhyssa snapped, coming to the cockpit door. Her hands were black with grease. 'When Crate says we're working as fast as we can, then we're –'

'Quiet,' Auric said, holding up a hand.

Rhyssa's face reddened. 'Don't you tell me to – wait, what's that noise?'

A hiss had begun to fill the cockpit, seeming to come from all around them. For a moment Lina was perplexed. Had something gone wrong with the ship?

Then she remembered the incident in the tunnel, that strange moment when the walls had seemed to speak.

'Hffrr?' she asked. 'Is that you?'

'*It issssss . . .*' the Agarian's voice was faint, but growing clearer. 'Are you ready to lifffft offfff?'

Milo reached up to touch a patch of black fungus on the wall. The fungus vibrated beneath his fingers. Lina saw another patch on the console, and a larger one on the floor beneath the pilot's seat.

'We're almost there,' Auric said, not sure which direction to talk in.

'Good,' Hffrr said. 'Your ship should not be damaged when it happens, but you should make yourselves as secure as possible.'

'When what happens?' Milo asked. 'What are you up to?'

Hffrr laughed silkily. 'Young Milo,' he

said. 'I will miss your curious mind. Very well, since we have a moment to spare. You call us Agarians, but this world is not our true home. We colonised it the same way you humans would colonise an uninhabited world. When I first arrived, Agaris was nothing but a rock. All the life you see around you came with us.'

'But how?' Milo asked. 'How did you travel here without ships?'

'In spores,' Hffrr explained. 'We are not like you, we do not require oxygen to survive, only a little light. We can survive in the vacuum, journeying long and far until we find a world fit for our needs. Then we settle, and this is the result.'

'Wait, go back,' Auric said. 'You said, when you first arrived. But it must have taken thousands of years for all this life to flourish. How old are you, Hffrr?'

The Agarian laughed again. 'We do not measure time the way you do,' he said. 'But I have seen stars born and die.'

There was a sudden, low rumble, and Lina felt the ground beneath them shake.

'It has begun,' Hffrr said. 'It is time for you to leave.'

'We're ready,' CR-8R's voice called from the back of the ship. 'The connections are secure. I can make the final repairs to the hyperdrive once we are in orbit.'

Rhyssa nodded. 'Good enough for me,' she said, strapping herself in beside Milo as the ship rattled around them. 'Let's get moving.'

'We will not see each other again,' Hffrr's disembodied voice said sadly. 'But it has been a joy getting to know all of you. Lina, be brave. Milo, keep exploring. Rhyssa and Auric, look after one another. If there's one thing I've learned in my long life, it's that family is the most important thing in the universe.'

'Thank you,' Auric said, firing up the engines. 'For everything.'

'We won't forget you,' Milo added.

'Goodbye, Hffrr,' Lina said. 'Thanks for saving us.'

'It wassss . . . my pleassssure . . . ' Hffrr hissed, as his voice faded away.

Auric hit the thrusters and the *Star Herald* began to lift. A wind was rising, Lina could feel it buffeting the ship as they ascended towards the clouds.

'What's happening?' Milo asked, peering out of the side window as the ship banked. The ground had begun to shift and shake, geological waves rippling outward across the planet's surface. As the earthquakes increased in intensity Lina saw the mountains beginning to subside, boulders tumbling into the plain below. The Imperial compound split open down the centre, smoke billowing out as the courtyard heaved and tipped. And at the centre of each wave was one of those massive new growths, a vast circular bowl of grey-green fungus with a dark opening in the centre.

'What *are* those things?' Milo asked as the *Star Herald* tore through the churning clouds. 'What are they d–'

There was a deafening WHOOMPH.

Agaris shook from pole to pole, as though a massive explosion had gone off in the heart of the planet. The *Star Herald* rattled, walls and windows vibrating. Through the glass Lina could see the entire world shudder, as though an invisible hand had taken hold and was shaking it roughly.

And like a giant puffball ejecting its seeds, Agaris shed its skin. The clouds shredded, billowing out into space. Lina saw the mushroom forest sloughing away from the planet's surface,

fountains of black earth churning up towards them. The great round caps tumbled and rolled, huge root systems dragging behind them. The slender stalks shot up like arrows, driven by the force of the earthquake. One of them swept towards the *Star Herald*, its bulbous head clipping the ship and knocking them aside.

'Get us out of here,' Rhyssa ordered as the cloud of debris swallowed them.

Auric nodded.

It was like steering through an asteroid field, Lina thought, except these projectiles were smaller and squashier, drifting outward into space. The ship would still suffer serious damage if one of the big ones slammed into them, though.

Then something shot past the viewport, travelling faster than any of the loose stalks. It was a black sphere half the size of the *Star Herald*, moving at blinding speed into the darkness beyond. Another followed, and another.

'It's them!' Milo said excitedly, craning his head to look back at the planet.

The black spheres came bursting from the centre of those giant funnels like bolts from an ion cannon, punching through the debris field and out into empty space. The planet shook with every violent discharge.

'What do you mean, them?' Auric asked, watching in wonder.

'The Agarians,' Milo said. 'These must be the seedlings Hffrr was talking about, the ones that can survive in space. Look, they're headed for the sun.'

He was right. The spores moved in formation, curving towards the distant star.

'Won't they burn up?' Lina wondered.

'They must use the star's gravity,' Rhyssa suggested. 'A slingshot, to give them speed. They need to cross interstellar distances, after all.'

'Okay, that's now the most awesome thing I've ever seen,' Milo said. 'Sorry, Crate.'

'Not at all,' the droid called from the hold. 'I quite agree.'

'Even the Empire are getting out of their way,' Auric said, and Lina saw the

Star Destroyer taking evasive action, angling out of Agaris's orbit as the debris cloud expanded towards it.

'Let's listen in,' Rhyssa said, flicking on the radio. Static filled the cockpit.

An Imperial voice broke through. '*Should we open fire?*'

'*Let them go,*' Tarkin replied in clipped tones. '*The planet is ours.*'

'*I'm picking up a ship leaving Agaris,*' the first voice continued. '*It's an Imperial craft, but all our ships are accounted for.*'

'*The Family Graf,*' Tarkin sneered. '*Good. Send a fighter squadron to intercept.*'

Rhyssa flicked off the radio. 'I really can't stand that man.' She turned, raising her voice. 'Crater, how's that hyperdrive coming along?'

'Almost there,' the droid replied. 'Two minutes.'

Lina saw four TIE fighters emerging from the *Executrix* and turning towards them. 'We might not have two minutes.'

'I'll plot a course,' Auric said, bending over the console. 'We can make the jump to light speed the second Crater gives the all-clear.'

'Do we know where we're going?' Rhyssa asked.

'Somewhere safe,' Auric said. 'We still have the maps, remember? We'll find a nice, quiet world, somewhere green and peaceful, far away from stormtroopers and Star Destroyers.'

An image flashed into Lina's head. A house in the woods, by a fast-flowing river. A plantation filled with lush, fruit-bearing plants. A place where she and Milo could grow up strong and healthy, where their parents could teach them all they needed to know to survive. Her whole family, together, light years from danger. It was perfect.

But it was impossible.

'No,' she said. 'No, we can't.'

Auric turned to her. 'What do you mean?' he asked. 'Lina, I won't put you both in danger again.'

Lina put her hand on his arm. 'The whole galaxy's in danger, Dad. The Empire won't stop until it's all theirs, every single world. And we won't be able to live with ourselves if we run away.'

'We're not running away,' Rhyssa argued. 'This isn't our fight.'

'It's everyone's fight,' Milo said, facing his mother. 'Lina's right. There are people out there who risked everything for us. We were lost and alone and we didn't know what we were doing, and they helped us. Now it's our turn to help them.'

'The rebels?' Auric asked. 'We'll never be able to thank them for all they did. But they chose to put their lives in danger. They made a decision to fight the Empire. We never had a choice.'

'But now we do,' Lina said. 'And we have to go back.'

'I agree.' CR-8R floated in the doorway, watching them.

Rhyssa looked up. 'You too, Crate?' she asked. 'You're programmed to protect Milo and Lina, not lead them into danger.'

'That is not quite correct, Miss Rhyssa,' CR-8R said. 'If you recall, you were the one who installed my primary programming. You designed me to protect children, knowing that I would begin with yours. But Milo and Lina are not the only children in the galaxy. There are billions more under threat. The Empire do not care about children. They do not care about anything except power. If we join this fight, who knows how many lives we could save?'

For a moment there was silence. Lina looked from her mother's face to her father's. Auric's eyes were on the floor, and he was shaking his head slowly.

Then a laser blast slammed into the *Star Herald*'s side and Milo cried out. The TIEs screamed towards them, blasting as they rocketed overhead.

'Crater, I hope you fixed the hyperdrive before you decided to come and lecture us,' Rhyssa said.

'Of course,' the droid replied. 'And I also took the liberty of plotting a course for Lothal.'

Auric looked up at him. 'You did . . . what?'

Milo laughed. 'Crater, you're a genius.'

Another blast rocked the ship. Ahead of them, Lina could see the Agarian spores circling towards the sun, gleaming as they picked up speed. She hoped Hffrr and his people made it to safe harbour. But for her, there was no such place. It was time to go back and continue the fight.

'Punch it, Dad,' she said, reaching for Milo's hand and squeezing it tight.

Auric hit the hyperdrive. The stars streaked towards them, and they were gone.